IGNORANCE IS A PLEASANT EVIL

The ABC Files by Paul Masson

Ignorance is a Pleasant Evil

Paul Masson

ISBN 978-1-7382730-4-1
Publisher Paul Robert Masson, PO Box 1866, Niagara-on-the-Lake, ON L0S 1J0, Canada
First Printing, 2025

Acknowledgements

The characters in this book are fictitious, as is Wildcat Oil Services, and any resemblance to persons living or dead is purely coincidental. In contrast, the descriptions of the book's settings, in particular the Athabasca oil sands in Alberta and the Fort McKay First Nation, are intended to be accurate to the extent possible.

As always, I enjoy doing research. Part of the fun and challenge of writing books for me is to learn something along the way. In writing this book, I have relied on numerous sources, including the websites of the Alberta Energy Regulator, the government of Alberta, the Pembina Institute, Oil Sands Magazine, National Geographic, the Globe and Mail, the CBC, the Fort McKay First Nation, Alberta Native News, and many others. The *Science* journal article that found that carbon emissions were as much as 64 times those reported by the oil companies is He, M. *et al. Science* 383, 426–432 (2024).

The sayings about boating are taken from an article I wrote for the July 2024 issue of the Niagara-on-the-Lake Sailing Club's newsletter, *The Mainsheet,* entitled "Men and Boats: Lessons from the Sailing Life."

I am grateful to my wife Betsy and to the members of the Niagara-on-the-Lake Writers' Circle–especially Eileen Campbell, Carole McKinnon, and Kathryn Recourt–for helpful comments.

Preface

Ashcroft-by-the-Sea, on the South Shore of Nova Scotia's Atlantic coast, was founded in the late 18th century by United Empire Loyalists. It retains many of the handsome brick and stone houses built in its heyday, though the sources of its early prosperity, fishing and lumber industries, have long ago moved out or shut down. Now it's a retirement community, occasionally called ABC–chosen by wealthy retirees from as far away as Toronto as the place to spend their golden years in pleasant surroundings and to breathe a bracing sea air.

Hamish Cameron was one of those, having retired at the age of 75 as judge on Nova Scotia's Court of Appeals. However, circumstances led him to start a new career as a detective. He and Sean Carroll investigate some of the goings-on in their not always idyllic community. This is the account of the latest case of Cameron and Carroll, Investigators.

Ashcroft-by-the-Sea

1

Ashcroft-by-the-Sea

Hamish stood in the office in Sean's old family mansion, where their detective agency was housed, patting his pockets, looking for his key. *Damn, just another symptom of getting old. Every time I hear about Gen X or Gen Z, I realize how old I am. The alphabet wasn't even invented when I was born!*

Sean appeared with two mugs of coffee, offering one to Hamish. "Beth is starting with us full time today. She's smart and inquisitive–I'm sure she'll work out well, after we teach her the ropes." Hamish Cameron, a former judge, and Sean Carroll were partners in a detective agency, though Hamish was considering easing out.

Beth Phillips was Sean's new main squeeze. They had met when he investigated thefts of food provided to Halifax restaurants by the logistics firm where she worked. She quit her dead-end job to join Cameron and Carroll, Investigators, with the aim of becoming a private detective. She was about 15 years younger than Sean.

"You realize that Marjoree walked out when she heard we were hiring Beth. She was a great help keeping track of things at the agency, billing and such. So just because you wanted to hire your new girlfriend we have to do without an office manager who happens to be your former girlfriend."

"I'm sorry, these things happen. At my age, you have to listen to your heart!"

Hamish shrugged his shoulders, and changed the subject. "Let's see–what do we have to do today? I'm sure there was something related to that new client of ours–what's his name, Jeremy Boswell? Oh, I have it! He hired us to track down a distant cousin whom he hasn't seen since the horrific accident that killed the girl they were both sweet on when they were teenagers."

"You've got it, Hamish. This would be a good case to start Beth on, so she can learn on the job. Would you help her learn about how we go about locating people? You could take her through the various databases that we tap into."

"Sure. But she won't have the same access to contacts in the provincial government and the legal community that I have, you know."

"Hamish, you're the one who said you wanted to ease out of the detective business! Now you seem reluctant to train a successor. Let's give it a shot, see how she turns out. The two of you could share the workload if you don't want to retire completely."

"OK," Hamish said grudgingly. "Just be aware that Izzie and I are leaving for our vacation in BC in three weeks, so after that Beth will be your responsibility."

A knock at the door interrupted their conversation. Sean let Beth in, giving her a peck on the cheek. She brushed back her blond hair from her round, cheery face. "I'm excited–my first day at a new job! I'm really looking forward to this!"

She nodded to Hamish, who looked at her frostily without volunteering a greeting. He glanced at Sean, raising his eyebrows. Turning back to Beth, he said "OK then, let me start you on your first case."

2

"We can use the Nova Scotia Land Registry online, to see if this fellow, Thomas Boswell, owns property in the province. Since our client says that he and his cousin grew up in Cape Breton, that seems like a good place to start." Hamish showed Beth how to log on to the database. "The fee is modest, so it makes sense for the agency to subscribe to the service."

The search drew a blank. Beth asked, "What about social media? Shall we give that a try?" She typed in the name Thomas Boswell, and discovered that there were dozens with that name on each of the sites. "Doesn't Jeremy Boswell know whether his cousin still lives in the province? Did he go to university? Anything at all about his current whereabouts? What about his profession? If we had some of these we could filter out the names that don't fit."

Hamish nodded his head grudgingly. "You seem to be getting the hang of it. I'll let you get on with the job, then. Why don't I set up an interview for you with our client, and you can question him about his cousin? Then you can formulate a strategy for finding Thomas Boswell."

Beth smiled. "I'll try to pry more information out of Jeremy, but if that doesn't work, I'll have to go to Cape Breton to dig up what there is to know about him."

*****

Jeremy Boswell's house was an old Victorian mansion with gables and turrets, much like Sean's family homestead, The Oaks. It was located in the old part of Ashcroft-by-the-Sea, built in the 19th century, when the town was populated by successful businessmen in construction, lumber, and shipping. The industries had mainly moved away, with the exception of a pulp and paper plant, Morrisons, which was located far enough away not to disturb the wealthy inhabitants of the old town. Some of the original families still lived there, while other houses had been bought by newcomers like Boswell. A few had been torn down and replaced by townhouses.

While Beth walked to the Boswell residence, which was a mere two blocks away from The Oaks, for her 10 o'clock appointment, she rehearsed the questions she wanted to ask Jeremy. Hamish had only given her a sketchy summary of their earlier conversation. *I still don't understand exactly why, at this late date, Jeremy wants to make contact with Thomas Boswell. If he's the only surviving relative, surely he'll want to leave something to him anyway. Either that or give away his money to charity.*

The door was opened by an elderly lady wearing an apron. She smiled. "You must be Beth. Mr. Boswell told me to expect you. Please come on into the study." She led Beth down a long hallway with a high ceiling. "He'll be down shortly. In the meantime, can I bring you a cup of tea?"

Beth nodded her assent. "Awesome, I'd love one."

Dark oak bookcases lined the walls. A roll-top desk was open, loose pages spread on its writing surface. She glanced at the top page–*The Last Will and Testament of Jeremy Boswell, esq.* Before she could read more, footsteps sounded in the hall, and she quickly moved away from the desk.

Boswell was a painfully thin, tall, middle-aged man, with sinewy hands and a bony face. His mouth was twisted, as if he were attempting a smile but was only able to grimace. He strode over to her and shook her hand in a courtly manner. "It's a pleasure to meet you, Ms. Phillips. Please tell me how I can assist you."

"I was hoping you could give me some information on your cousin's background. Do you still speak or text with him? And if we locate him, what would you want us to find out about him? Or do you prefer us just to give you his contact details so you can talk to him yourself?"

"Er, well, I hadn't really thought about what to do next. Let me explain by giving you a little background. My folks settled near Orangedale in Nova Scotia in the early 19th century. My forebear Robert Boswell grew up in Scotland. We were farmers, mostly, until the Intercontinental Railway came to Cape Breton, building a station at Orangedale. That transformed the place into something more than a rural village, since the stop became an important access point to the area. Alexander Graham Bell often travelled to and from Baddeck via the Orangedale station. Tourists got off there to visit the Bras d'Or Lakes, and supplies of all kinds were loaded or unloaded at Orangedale. My father got a job as assistant station-master, while my mother made pies that were sold at a bakery located on the main street. It did a brisk business around the times that trains came through."

Beth put her hand over her mouth to stifle a yawn. "I'm with you so far."

"As a child, I used to play beside the railroad tracks with other local boys, including several of my cousins. My playmates and I had the train schedules engraved in our brains–it was second nature for us to make sure we didn't venture onto the tracks when the passenger express roared in just before noon, and when it made its return trip at four. We also knew to expect a freight train later in the afternoon bringing goods unloaded at the port of Sydney to Antigonish, New Glasgow, and points west. There was also the occasional slow-moving train bearing coal.

"I was an only child, but had a generally happy childhood. However, one event profoundly marked my teenage years and clouded the rest of my life. It happened just before I started grade eleven, at the end of summer."

Jeremy wiped his brow, and slumped lower in his chair.

"I was 'walking out' with a girl–as we said in those days–named Margaret Bartholomew. We were 16, and we were very close, though there was another boy who was courting her, my cousin Tom. His family looked after shipping produce to market, and supplying the seeds and supplies to locals. Thus, they were important people in town, relatively wealthy, and Tom thought himself a cut above me. Besides, he was a year older than I was.

"Things came to a head one spring day when I was walking home from school, holding hands with Margaret. Tom came along behind and told her that she could do better than me. 'He's just a silly sixteen-year-old. I'm going to study business in Halifax and take over from my father in a few years.' I didn't know what to say, so I said nothing. Tom taunted me again: 'He's just a yellow belly, Margaret. I'll bet you I can stay on the tracks longer than him when the express comes back from Sydney.'

"We both knew that the train was due in a few minutes. He was challenging me to stand in the middle of the tracks and jump off at the last minute as the locomotive sped towards the station. Normally I was not stupid enough to play that game but now my blood was up.

"'Don't do it,' Margaret wailed. I should have listened to her but Tom had challenged my bravery and I couldn't back down. So both of us stood side-by-side between the rails, waiting for the train to appear on the bridge at Grand Narrows. A single blast of the train horn announced its imminent arrival at the station. As the train came into view at the last bend before the station, the horn sounded a continuous wail as the engineer attempted to clear the track.

"Neither Tom nor I moved as the train approached, its brakes making a mournful crescendo of sound as it decelerated. I was determined to see Tom jump first, and the same was true on his part. I could see the train fill my field of vision, then a violent blow knocked both me and Tom off the track.

"It was Margaret. She could not stand by and see us get killed. She had thrown herself against us to push us out of the path of the train. But she had left it too late. She knocked us off the tracks, but had fallen in front of the train herself. The train could not stop in time. She was killed instantly."

Beth shook her head. "Oh My God, that's awful!" She was silent for several moments in shock, imagining what it must have been like to have been there. "What a thing to have happen! I can see how this memory could have haunted the rest of your life! But why do you want to find Tom? For revenge, or to make peace with him?"

"I don't know. I have to think it through. But first I need to know what's become of him."

She murmured, "What happened then?"

"Both Tom and I became outcasts. Our friends wouldn't talk to us anymore. People pointed me out on the street if I walked in town. I could have died of shame; I should have been dead, instead of Margaret.

"After a few months, I left Orangedale, and never lived there again. I was good at figures, and my parents got me into an accounting program in Halifax. After graduating, I was accepted as an intern at an accounting firm there, then a full time employee, and later the chief accountant at a financial firm, Atlantic Venture Capital, from which I eventually retired as its senior vice president. By that time, my parents had died, as well as their generation of Boswells in Orangedale and most of my cousins. I don't know what happened to Thomas. My parents refused to talk to me about the terrible tragedy. Later, when I started wondering about him, I had lost touch with everyone I had known as a youth, so I couldn't ask anyone there."

Beth thought for a moment before replying. "I can start by interviewing people in the town. Someone will know where he's gone, if he no longer lives in the area. But what shall I say to them—that you want to put him in your will?"

"You don't understand. I've spent most of my life refusing to think about the horrible thing that happened that day on the train tracks, while at the same time having the memory burned into me so that I couldn't rid myself of it. Now that I am getting old, I want to make peace with that event. Locating Thomas and finding out whether his life was similarly affected would be a big part of it. It might tell me if my life could have been different. I never married, never had close friendships. Margaret's death hardened me, stunted my ability to feel emotions. Perhaps Thomas has been the same way. I'd like to know one way or another."

"Then what do you want us to do if we find him?"

"Let me know what you learn. Perhaps then I can decide what to do next."

3

Orangedale

"So you want to go to Orangedale, do you?" Hamish asked. "I guess you're the best person. Sean's busy, and I'm not too keen on field work these days. Boswell told us he'll pay expenses. But you'll need to keep receipts. That's the first law of detective work: always keep receipts! The second one is: don't believe what they tell you–always check it out with some independent source. Everyone has their angle, and they're trying to tilt the table so the dice roll their way."

"OK, Philip Marlowe. I think I've learned the ropes now. Thanks for your tutoring!"

"Oh, and don't forget Sam Spade's code, when he explains to Brigid O'Shaughnessy in the *Maltese Falcon* why he's sending her up the river to Sing-Sing: 'When a man's partner is killed, he's supposed to do something about it.' You can adjust the pronoun to suit your own circumstances! Hopefully none of us will get killed, though!"

*****

It was a long drive from Ashcroft to Orangedale. Beth stopped to pick up some clothes and toiletries at her apartment in Dartmouth, then drove north to Cape Breton Island. There were bushes in bloom on this mild early-July day. She was happy, speeding along in her little Mazda Miata with the windows open, the wind brushing back her blond hair. She got a few admiring looks from people–mostly men–along her path.

Beth thought back to her carefree days at Eastern University, when she had friends with cars who invited her to explore the countryside with them. When their studies and the weather allowed, they would go to Cape Breton, necessarily taking the Canso Causeway just as she was doing today. They would often kayak on the Bras D'Or Lakes or hike along the shore. After eating lobster rolls at a roadside pub, they would drive back to their university lodgings.

She had grown up as an only child in a modest two-bedroom home in Dartmouth. Her father worked in a shipyard as a welder while her mother stayed home. She did well in school, earning a provincial scholarship to university. She started out studying English literature, imagining that some day she would write novels. Then reality set in as she realized that she would have to find a paying job in the meantime. She took an interest in environmental science, and became convinced that something had to be done to reverse the planet's dependence on fossil fuels. However, she decided that she couldn't afford a career that required a postgraduate degree. She switched to the business curriculum, graduating eventually with a B.Comm.

Getting an employer to take her on a few years after the Great Recession was not easy. She received one offer, assistant to the marketing manager of a logistics company in Halifax, and took the job. Atlantic Food Services delivered meat, fish, and produce to local restaurants. While her salary paid her living expenses at the small flat in downtown Dartmouth where she now lived, she soon realized that there were few possibilities for advancement and after two years she had learned all there was to know about the job. She stayed on while exploring other options, which were few. Hence she jumped at the chance to join Cameron and Carroll, Investigators, as a junior detective. She met Sean Carroll while he was investigating thefts from AFS trucks, and they hit it off. At this stage in her life, she was open to new adventures.

After crossing the Canso Causeway Beth continued on the TransCanada for another forty-odd kilometres to Iron Mines, where she turned onto Orangedale Road and drove the remaining five kilometres to her destination. She had researched the town and surrounding areas on the Internet. There wasn't much to Orangedale now that the railroad no longer ran, but the old station was now a railway museum so she stopped in there. Beth said good morning to a woman about her age who was sitting behind a desk at the entrance, going through a list of items in the museum's collection. "Do you know anyone named Boswell around here? I'm looking for a certain Thomas Boswell, but I don't know if he still has folks in the area."

"I'm not from here, I'm afraid. But you could ask at the general store. It's just around the corner."

Beth first walked around the old station, which was still laid out as for its original purpose, with ticket counters and benches for those waiting for their train. She glanced at the exhibits. She noted that a certain George Boswell was listed among the station masters. *I'll bet that's Jeremy's father.* After taking a few pictures of the rail cars outside, she walked a hundred metres to the general store. Like its quaint name, it was a throwback to an earlier era. It carried a wide variety of items crammed into a small space, a sort of mini big-box store from long ago.

"Tom Boswell, you say? Of course I remember him. He even worked here during a summer, what, 30 years ago? At least. Anyway, he's been gone for a long time now. He worked at managing the family farm for a few years, decided that it wasn't his thing, and headed out west. He said he would discover his true calling by moving around and trying various careers. He figured he could always find a job in mining or oil drilling in Alberta or BC. I don't know if he ever settled down. I heard about him from time to time from his parents at first, but they passed away two decades ago."

Beth shook her head in disappointment. "Is there anyone else in town who might have kept in touch or know his whereabouts?"

"The town pretty much cleared out after passenger service stopped in 1990. It's no longer a place people come to as tourists, and it's too far from Sydney to make it a commuter town. To be sure, some stayed on after the trains stopped, but they were the old folks, and most have died off by now. There are a lot of empty houses. But you might try Sarah Bartholomew, she lives by herself now in a farmhouse a few kilometres out of town."

Beth gasped. "Bartholomew–that's the name of the girl who died in the train crash!"

He scowled. "You know about that, do you? Why are you digging up old stories? What is it you're doing here? Are you from the media?"

Beth shook her head. "No, you don't understand, I'm not a reporter! I'm trying to locate Thomas Boswell on behalf of his cousin Jeremy. He told me about her awful death. He wants to get back in touch with Tom."

"Oh, I see. Jeremy, now he's trying to make contact with his folks again? He hasn't set foot in town in decades. I don't remember much about him. He was a serious boy, not like that Tom. I felt sorry for him, you know. It wasn't his fault, but he paid the price. OK, go see Margaret's mother then, but I doubt she'll say much to you. And she didn't want to have anything to do with the two boys, Tom and Jeremy, after what happened to her daughter."

*****

Beth drove up the long driveway leading to the farmhouse. She noticed that it was badly in need of paint. *That's probably the least of its problems.* The roof was missing shingles in places, and one of the window openings had a plywood sheet nailed over it. The lawn was overgrown with weeds and had not been mown in a long time.

Beth used the brass knocker attached to the centre of the solid white wooden door. After a minute a raspy voice inside asked, "Whaddya want?"

"Mrs. Bartholomew? I'm trying to find someone who used to live in Orangedale."

"Oh, yeah. Who?"

"Tom Boswell."

"Don't ask me about that good-for-nothing no-account. He got my girl killed! Besides, I don't know anything about his whereabouts, I haven't seen him in ages. Now go away."

Beth heard footsteps receding from the door. She shrugged her shoulders, turned and walked back to her car. *So much for my one lead.* She drove back into the town, passing the general store and stopping in front of a white clapboard house with an iron fence and a gate that led from the street to the front door. *At least it looks well maintained, so I bet someone's living here.*

Before she had time to ring the bell, the door opened and a cheery woman of about fifty bade her good afternoon. "How can I help you?"

"I'm trying to locate Thomas Boswell, who used to live in town but apparently no longer does. Do you know anything about him?" Beth was doubtful the woman would have known him before he left town, but it was worth a try.

"Well, now. As it happens this is the house that the Boswell family used to own. I never met Tom but I heard about him from his parents, when we bought their house a little over twenty years ago. So why don't you come in? I can look through the correspondence I had with them shortly after we moved in. Perhaps that can help you. Would you like a cup of tea? My name is Mary Sawyer, by the way."

They had tea at a dining table with a white lace tablecloth, overlooking a garden with a riot of colour from peony and rose bushes. Mary sat back, giving a contented sigh. "It's nice chatting with you, Beth. The town is very quiet, and I don't often get visitors. Would you like a biscuit with your tea?"

"Sure, that would be amazing. I didn't eat any lunch." She looked around the room while Mary brought home-baked tea biscuits from the kitchen. There were souvenirs from long-ago vacations and family photos, but none seemed to include the Boswells. Beth asked her, "Do you have any idea where the Boswells moved to after selling their house to you?"

"Let me dig out the correspondence I had with them." Mary went into her bedroom and brought out a cardboard box with letters and house sale documents, which she spread on the table. Mary leafed through them. "Let's see, the first letter I got from them was sent from Calgary, but that was just a temporary place for Tom's parents, Dorothy and John. They wanted to be close to Tom, but he hadn't settled down yet. He was working on oil rigs, and went where the job took him, usually living in a place with other roughnecks at the company's expense. So his parents bought an RV out there and were driving around, seeing the sights in the meantime. They asked me to forward their mail to various places on their route. Here's a letter with a later date that says they were planning to keep going west. They thought they would at least go over the pass into BC, drive down the Fraser valley, and visit Vancouver. I remember that the last mail I received for them here I forwarded to general delivery at the main Vancouver postal station. I never heard anything more from them after that."

"Do you remember any details about the company where Tom worked then? Maybe they would still have contact info for him."

"It was Wildcat Oil Services, I think. He might still be there, for all I know."

"It's worth a try. And thanks for talking to me."

Back in Ashcroft, Beth reported back to Hamish. "Sorry I don't have more to show for my trip to Orangedale. I'll try the oil services company where he worked, which is head-quartered in Calgary. Maybe I'll get lucky."

Hamish shrugged his shoulders. "Well, in this business you can't expect results right away, Beth. Keep digging. Just be aware that if you go out to Alberta, they require private investigators to be licensed, unlike Nova Scotia. You may be OK if you're just there temporarily. I would keep a low profile, though."

4

Calgary

The flight to Calgary was full. Beth dragged her rollaboard suitcase down the centre aisle of the Airbus A320, and ended up taking a middle seat near to the back. The man seated at the aisle didn't offer to help her put her suitcase in the overhead compartment, but instead checked out her body as she strained to get the bag between much larger suitcases that were already in the bin.

Once seated, she was treated to an obvious attempt to chat her up. "Are you from Calgary? I hear that the fires up north are sending smoke down into the city."

Beth shrugged her shoulders and said, "I don't know," before turning to her book, the latest Michael Connelly novel. She ignored her neighbour's attempt to continue the conversation. *It's going to be a long flight, and I don't want to have to chit chat with the jerk.*

She'd had to justify the trip to Hamish. "Wildcat Oil Services refused to discuss personnel issues on the phone with me, so I have to fly out to visit them in person. It'll be worth it if

I get them to give me Tom Boswell's employment status and contact information. If that doesn't pan out, I've found several people with that name who live in northeastern Alberta. I can check them out to see if one of them is the one we're looking for."

Hamish looked sceptical. "You're going to need to get Jeremy's go-ahead first and make sure that he will finance the trip."

That had proved surprisingly easy. He had just insisted, should she be successful in locating Tom, that she should gather as much info as possible without alerting him to the fact that Jeremy had hired her. He didn't want Tom to try to sweet talk himself into his will until he'd made up his mind what he wanted to do.

In the meantime, Beth did some research into Alberta's oil sector. She learned that Alberta became a major producer of conventional oil with the discovery of Leduc No. 1 well in 1947. Exploitation of much larger reserves of unconventional oil–the oil sands–did not begin for another two decades. In 1967, the Great Canadian Oil Sands, a subsidiary of the US Sun Oil Company, began surface mining of bitumen near Fort McMurray. Those deposits, known as the Athabasca oil sands, are by far Canada's largest source of heavy oil, but Alberta's Peace River and Cold Lake oil sands are also significant producers. At present, surface mining continues, but new production has largely come from deeper deposits, where steam is used to liquify the bitumen, and then the oil is pumped out. Canada's output of both conventional and unconventional oil now exceeds 5 million barrels per day, making it the fourth largest producer in the world, after the United States, Saudi Arabia, and Russia.

During the flight, she thought about the line she should take with Thomas Boswell if she was able to locate him. *I don't want to give away the fact that it's his cousin who's looking for him. But I need to give him an incentive to talk to me—something to his advantage. Perhaps a class action suit against his employer? I think I'll have to play it by ear until I know more about him.*

She took a cab to the Sheraton, and after checking in, walked to The Bow, an office tower where Wildcat Oil Services had its head office. She took the elevator up to the 30th floor and entered their offices through a glass door. There was a small lobby leading to an open floor plan of desks, where men and women stared at their computer screens or spoke on the phone. The entrance did not have a receptionist, but after a minute a young man at a desk came over to ask Beth what she wanted.

"I'd like to speak to someone in your HR department, please."

"You can go down there and knock at the door with 'Human Resources' painted on it." He pointed to a hallway leading off of the large open room. "Do you have an appointment?"

"No, I was just told to stop in."

He nodded, then went back to his desk, leaving her to find her way to HR down a corridor with beige wall-to-wall carpeting. The walls, which were painted a similar colour, were unadorned with anything that would break the monotony.

The windowless door did not allow Beth to see inside, so after knocking she opened it and walked up to a long counter that separated the entranceway from the offices. A woman was seated at the counter, behind a box labelled "Leave Applications Here." She was leafing through them, but looked up and said, "You'll be notified by mail when a decision is made on your application."

"No, no. I'm not an applicant. I'm trying to locate one of your employees, or perhaps a former employee. I need to contact him about an inheritance." She told herself this was only a small lie–it might even be true.

"We're not allowed to give out that sort of information. We're obliged by law to respect the privacy of our employees."

Beth put on her most earnest expression. "You're the only lead I have. Thomas Boswell worked for you a number of years ago, that's all I know. Can't you at least tell me if he's still an employee, or, if not, if you still have his contact information? I could leave you a letter for him–you wouldn't have to give me his address."

"Very well, I guess I can do that. But with no guarantee that the letter will get to him. Here, I'll give you an envelope and some note paper."

Beth wrote a short letter, addressed to Thomas Boswell, care of Wildcat Oil Services, asking him to contact her about a matter to his financial advantage and giving her cell phone number. Putting it in an envelope with his name on it labelled 'Private and Confidential,' she handed it to the woman. "That should do it. I hope you can get it to him quickly, because I'm only in Calgary for a few days."

Back in her hotel room, Beth considered her next steps while she waited. She decided to do a more thorough search of social media, starting with LinkedIn. She found a Thomas Boswell with experience in the oil exploration industry who was located in Fort McMurray, the city in northern Alberta that serviced the Athabasca Oil Sands. A massive forest fire had nearly destroyed it in 2016. *Not a very pleasant place to live, or even to visit. But I may have to go up there if I don't receive a response to my letter soon.*

5

Fort McMurray

The De Havilland Dash-8 prepared for landing in Fort Mc-Murray after the hour-and-a-half flight from Calgary. The pilot announced that they were forced to modify their flight path because of smoke from the wildfires. Looking out the window as they circled, Beth gasped at the desolation of the Athabasca oil sands. She saw that broad swaths of land had been stripped of all vegetation and mined for the bitumen, leaving only huge ruts in the black soil. On the horizon was an enormous plant that belched smoke, while in the foreground was a large lake, which she assumed was a tailings pond that contained contaminated water left over from the mining process. *The plant must be either where the mined bitumen is upgraded, or where they generate the steam for injecting into the in situ deposits. What an awful sight!* She was appalled by the post-apocalyptic sight of devastation. *How can they be allowed to do this?*

As best she could judge, the other passengers were either here on business or returning home. There were few tourists. Beth understood that Fort McMurray had begun life as a fur-trading post, but that at present it existed almost solely to service the oil sands. Accordingly, available jobs were limited to those in the oil business and supporting activities. *At least it's easy to get through the airport,* she thought. She was in a rental car 15 minutes after getting off the plane, driving toward downtown.

She checked into the Pomeroy Hotel, which she'd been told was the best and most central hotel in town. She wanted to be able to walk to places.

She picked up her key at the front desk and went up to her second-floor room. It was nowhere near as nice as the one at the Sheraton in Calgary. After unpacking she decided to go for a walk.

The street where someone with the name Thomas Boswell was supposed to live was lined with narrow prefab houses and trailers on concrete blocks. There was scarcely room for grass on each lot so most of them sported just dirt and gravel, and the occasional stunted tree. Number 16 Palliser Place was no different. It was hard to tell whether it was occupied or vacant.

There was a newspaper and a few letters scattered on a concrete step leading to the front door. They seemed to be utility bills, and were addressed to Thomas Boswell. No personal mail. *This isn't getting me very far. I'll have to see if he's home, and somehow figure out how to tell if it's the Thomas Boswell we're looking for or not.*

She rang the bell, which didn't seem to work, so she rapped on the front door. She thought she heard movement inside so she rapped again. A man in a tee shirt and jeans opened the door, with several days of stubble on his face. He was lean and frail, and wheezed from the effort of opening the door. Beth thought he could be from the same gene pool as Jeremy, but wasn't sure. "Thomas Boswell? I've come to see you about a class action suit against Wildcat Oil Services, aka WOS, by current and former employees."

The man said, "And who are you?"

"My name is Beth Phillips. I'm a private investigator hired by the lawyers filing the suit."

He seemed to accept that explanation, nodding his head. "You sent me a letter, didn't you? I never got around to calling you. So what's the beef against Wildcat? It's related to the emissions from the wells–right?"

Beth eagerly agreed with his assumption, and made up a story on the fly. "That's correct. Now, have you had respiratory problems that started while you were working for them? Could we start by telling me the dates you worked for the company?" She pulled out a clipboard from her cloth bag and stood by the steps, looking up at him expectantly.

The man confirmed that his full name was Thomas Bailey Boswell, and that he had worked at WOS for 18 years before retiring. He was suffering from emphysema. The symptoms had started after about 10 years on the job. "I complained to them that I couldn't do the work of a roughneck any longer. They gave me another job dealing with paperwork, but after another few years I'd had enough. I got them to give me a small pension because of my lung problems, and since then I've been working at a non-profit that monitors the work of the oil companies here. The wildfires don't help my breathing, and I shoulda moved somewhere else, but I can't afford to. My house here is paid for, and if I sold it for the chicken feed it would fetch I'd never be able to buy another place."

"So what was wrong with the air when you worked for WOS?"

"I dunno exactly, but I heard some of the guys saying that the PM2.5 emissions were a lot higher than they should be. Apparently oil sands extraction dumps a lot more pollution into the air than the industry claims–it's an open secret now. Anyway, isn't that what your suit is all about? You must know all that!" He looked at her sceptically.

"Oh, right! But I'm not an expert when it comes to the medical problems created by the oil sands. My job is to locate people who want to be part of the lawsuit." Thinking fast, Beth added: "So if you'll just tell me the best way to contact you, I'll send you the complete details about the suit and a form for you to sign if you want to be a part of it. Also, we'll need to know your next of kin. Do you have family here?"

"Naw. I came to Alberta more than 20 years ago from Nova Scotia and got the job at WOS after working at a couple of other oil services companies. My folks moved out too, but they're long dead now. There's just my daughter Claire, who lives here with me."

Beth thought, *I guess that's the proof I needed.* Turning to Tom, she said, "No problem, it was just that if you had other relatives here they could be part of the lawsuit also."

"I dunno about signing any form. I've got to look over what they got me to agree on when they gave me my pension. I might lose it if I sue."

"OK, We'll be in touch."

*****

Back at the hotel, Beth called Hamish. "I've found our man. Thomas Bailey Boswell is now retired from an oil services company in Fort McMurray on a disability pension. He's living in pretty basic housing here and is just getting by. So, do you think we should get back to Jeremy with the information, or do I keep digging? It'll be hard for me to get more info from Tom because I made up a story about a lawsuit against the company he used to work for. He'll probably have a ton of questions for me if I show up again."

"OK, that's a start. I'd suggest that you call Jeremy and report what you found, and ask him what you should do now. I suspect he'll want you to dig up more details of Tom Boswell's life, since you're there."

Jeremy was enthusiastic. "He works at Wildcat Oil Services, you say? That's strange, because the firm I worked for, Atlantic Venture Capital, helped launch the company! It was a great opportunity to take a stake in Canada's fastest growing industry. Anyway, you did a good job locating him. But I still don't know more about Tom than that he's a retired oil services worker and he's hard up."

"What more would you like to know?"

"I'd like you to find out what sort of life he's been leading. Perhaps talk to his co-workers at WOS, if there are any still there who worked with him? What about his daughter? What does she do?"

"How long would you like me to stay?"

I'll be happy to pay for you to spend two more days in Fort McMurray. See what you can dig up in that time. Oh, by the way: is the air quality OK there? I hear there's another wildfire burning north of the Athabasca oil sands."

"There always seems to be something in the air here, even when the smoke from the wildfires blows in another direction. I'm having trouble breathing. I'm told the oil companies under-report their emissions. Apparently an independent study came up with much higher figures than the ones the Alberta Energy Regulator reports."

"Yes, I heard that some people claim that it's unhealthy there. But I think that the environmental concerns are overblown. Let's face it, we still need the oil, and we might as well get it from Alberta rather than importing petroleum from the US or Saudi Arabia. It's one of the few things of value that Canada produces and exports in large quantities. Demand for fossil fuels isn't going away, even if we move to electric cars, trucks, and buses. We're still going to need petrochemicals and plastics and jet fuel–you're not going to want to fly in an electric plane! Besides, electrifying all vehicles would put too great a demand on the electrical grid, one that's not going to be met by renewables."

"Whatever you say, boss! Anyway, I'll do some more investigating and get back to you the day after tomorrow."

After the call was over, Beth did some more Internet research into the oil companies operating around Fort McMurray. She learned that all the big Canadian names had operations there: Imperial Oil, Suncor, Canadian Natural Resources, Syncrude, and Cenovus, as well as a host of smaller producers and oil service companies, including Wildcat Oil Services.

6

B eth located the local office of WOS without too much difficulty using Google Maps. She drove up Alberta 63, getting an occasional glimpse of the open pit mines, where the topsoil and boreal forest growth had been removed in order to mine the bitumen, load it onto giant trucks, and take it to a processing facility where it was liquified. She stopped a few times to take pictures. Most of the mining sites were hidden behind trees and berms, however, and not visible from the road.

The WOS office was a one story metal-clad building. A few cars were parked on a gravel lot in front of it, while in back there were trucks loaded with supplies and with equipment mounted on them. Before approaching the front door, Beth took some more photos.

As she was doing so, a burly man dressed in khaki work pants and jacket, and wearing heavy boots, came around the corner of the building. He strode up to her. "What are you doing? This is private property. Do you have any business here?"

Beth stood her ground. "I was hoping to talk to someone about a former employee, Tom Boswell. Did you know him?"

"What if I did? What business is that of yours?"

"I've been trying to locate him, because he may be entitled to a legacy from a cousin of his."

"Oh, yeah? I've heard that one before. Anyway, I don't know where he lives. I've lost touch."

"Is there anyone here who knows him well? Someone willing to talk to me?"

"All right, you can go inside and talk to Flora. He was her boss when he was heading the office that does procurement."

The front door led to a stuffy hall with a low ceiling. Doors to offices were visible on both sides. She headed down the hall, looking at names on the door. When she reached one with the name Flora Rivera, she knocked.

A deep female voice with a Hispanic accent said "Come in!" Inside was a woman behind a desk who looked a few years older than Beth. She had a tangle of dark hair and a brown face, which was devoid of makeup or any adornment except for a star tattoo on her left cheek. "*Allo?*" she said, looking up from a catalogue of industrial equipment.

"Hi, my name is Beth Phillips. I'm trying to get some info about Tom Boswell. I gather he used to work here?"

The woman looked at Beth dubiously. "*Que pasa?* Is he in some kind of trouble?"

"No way! Some old guy who's a distant relative wants to know more about him before deciding whether to put him into his will."

"Yeah, he used to work here, but he left a coupla years ago. He was an OK guy. What else do you want to know?"

"Did he have any close friends? What did he like to do with his time off?"

"Naw. He was a loner, except for spending a lot of time with his daughter. I think he made model trains as a hobby. He used to bring a miniature locomotive or a club car in for me to admire."

"I understand he had problems with his lungs. Is that why he left?"

"Yeah, he told me he got some payoff from the company. He'd threatened to sue them, and they gave in. Claimed that they were violating safety standards. The company won't admit it, but I know it's true. They make up the emissions data. The real numbers are a lot higher."

The office door had been left open and there was the sound of footsteps in the hall. Flora picked up the catalogue she'd been consulting. "Gotta get back to work."

"Can I get your phone number so that I can contact you again if I need to?"

Flora hurriedly scribbled it on a post-it note, which she passed to Beth just as a man wearing grey slacks and a sports jacket came into her office. Frowning, he looked Beth over before turning his back to her and speaking to Flora. "I need you to order that piping, and we need it to get here ASAP."

Beth slipped out and walked back to her car. Instead of driving directly back to her hotel, she decided to explore and take some more pictures. A service road led towards an oil sands mining site. She parked in front of a fence around its perimeter, and took photos of the vast wasteland left by the mining operation. She shuddered at its ugliness and the absence of any vegetation or wildlife for miles around. Even birds found no reason to visit it.

As she was about to get into her car and drive back, she noticed dust raised by a car speeding toward her. The jeep, with a flashing light on its roof and the inscription "Wildcat Oil Services" on its door, screeched to a stop. A man in a guard's uniform jumped out. "You can't come here! This is off limits!" He reached to his belt and unsnapped the cover on his holster.

Beth cowered. "Sorry, I got lost," she blurted. "I guess I have to head back to the main road the way I came." She quickly got back in her car and drove off, while looking in her rear-view mirror as the guard who was driving two car-lengths behind kept pace with her until she turned onto the highway.

7

"What's going on here, Sean? They're destroying the planet, and no one is doing anything about it! Maybe it's because it's so far from everything, nobody gives a shit. I feel I just have to keep digging for information about the place, write a story for an environmental magazine, organize a protest–do something!"

"Hold on there Beth. Breathe deeply. Your job is to find out about Thomas Boswell, not save the world! Just stick to the script, and give Jeremy the info he requested. Isn't that what Hamish has told you to do?"

"Sure. But I can't just ignore this."

"So, what do you propose to do?"

"I could stick around for a few more days and poke into what's going on with the tar sands, at my own expense. I promise I'll tell Jeremy Boswell what I've dug up about his cousin Tom. But I'll also gather the dirt I need to expose the oil sands–what used to be called the tar sands before the PR guys got involved."

"I don't think you should. But if you do, at least try to get Hamish onside first. He wasn't very happy with my signing you up in the first place. This is going to turn him even more against you."

"I'll do my best to keep Jeremy and Hamish happy. But that can't be as important as finding out more about this clusterfuck of the fossil-fuel era!"

*****

It was Saturday afternoon, so Beth thought it was OK to call Flora on her cell phone. It rang five times, and she was about to give up, when Flora answered. *"Hola, Que pasa?"*

"Flora, this is Beth again. I visited you at your office yesterday. Tell me what you meant when you said that WOS falsifies their emissions data. How can they do that?"

"Listen, Beth. I don't wanna talk about this on the phone. Are you in downtown Fort McMurray? We could meet at Earls Kitchen at seven. You know where that is?"

"I'll find it. See you then."

Earls turned out to be only a few blocks from her hotel, so Beth walked to it. The blank-faced concrete buildings made her uneasy. The restaurant and bar were in a nondescript structure that looked like a warehouse or an auto repair shop. It was flanked by the headquarters of a trade union for oil sands workers. Beth wandered into the restaurant a little after seven, ignored the receptionist, and looked for Flora, who waved from a table located across from the entrance that was located on a ledge above the main floor. Beth had to ford a large pool of tables before reaching steps that led to her roost against the far wall.

Flora had smartened up relative to her appearance at WOS. Her hair was neatly combed and she sported a blouse and harem pants. She had a glass of white wine in front of her. "Sit down, Beth. It'll get busy here after a while. A nice place to meet *caballeros*. Let's have dinner in the meantime."

Beth was taken aback. "I don't know about meeting guys, Flora. I just want to find out about Tom Boswell. But sure, let's have dinner. I'm starving."

A server came over and they ordered dinner, roast beef sliders for Flora and pulled chicken for Beth.

"So what do you want to know? And are you really just locating Tom for a cousin of his? You're an actual detective?"

"That's right, but I'm also interested in what life is like here. This place looks post-apocalyptic! All those scars carved into the earth, and the air doesn't feel right. I find myself gasping for breath."

"Yeah, that's the way it is. But the pay is pretty good, so I get to send some *dinero* to my family in Mexico. I just wish they would clean up the air here. The oil companies gotta file reports on the various forms of emissions that they pollute the air with, and figures on their carbon footprint. That's one of the services that WOS provides. My company has been giving low-ball pollution estimates for years and nobody has called us out. I'm sure they're doing this with the encouragement of the industry itself. We're a convenient tool for the oil producers because it allows them to pretend that they've obtained an arms-length assessment."

"So it's not just different equipment that gives the different estimates? I read that the industry uses a bottom-up approach while new studies that come up with much higher figures are top-down. Apparently they rely on aircraft collection of all pollutants, so they may include a lot of stuff that doesn't get counted in the oil company figures."

"*Si, si*, that's true, but the differences are so great that something smells about the numbers that the industry puts out. Maybe there are so many tiny emissions that they're ignored, but they add up to a lot. I hear that the emissions collected by aircraft are 60 times greater than our figures. Anyway, oil companies have always lied about their environmental impact. That's what they do–just like cigarette companies and the health risk of smoking."

"Flora, what can we do about it? Everyone who's not a climate change denier knows that Canada needs to reduce emissions drastically. It's committed to stringent targets. If the oil sands can't help meet them, then they should be shut down!"

"Whoa! It's way too big a business to shut down! It pays me and everybody else here good money. Sure, I wish they'd clean up their act. But hey, we've all got to make a living. You shut down the oil sands, all those big companies, Suncor, Canadian Natural Resources, Imperial Oil, and the rest would lose billions in revenue. Their stocks would plummet, and a lot of pension funds would be wiped out! The Alberta government lives on oil revenues and it isn't going to allow anyone to kill the goose that lays its golden eggs! There's just too much money involved. You go up against these guys, then they'll find a way to destroy you. So don't touch it!"

"I got you. Let's talk of something else. What do you do here for fun?"

"It's a great town for a single girl. Mostly of the population are guys, so not much competition! I'm not looking for a husband, just to have a good time. Don't have much problem doing that on a Saturday night. There are a lotta young bucks, rough-necks, who are working off some steam on weekends. And come Monday, all is forgotten, and it's back to the grind. That works for me."

"What about Tom? What's he do with his spare time?"

"He spends a lot of time with his daughter, Claire. He married an indigenous woman up in Fort McKay. Sadly, his wife died of some cancer or other, and he ended up having to raise the girl himself. She grew up living with him in Fort McMurray, went to university in Edmonton, I think, and now works for an environmental NGO in town which is campaigning to stop further exploitation of the oil sands."

"Any idea what the name of the NGO is?"

"Can't remember. Something with 'climate' and 'oil sands' in it. Google it, it should come up."

A man in his thirties with a deep tan and wearing shiny leather cowboy boots came over and said hello. "You ladies looking for company?" He nodded over to a table with another outdoors type sitting quietly but looking their way. "Me and my pal are planning to go over to Rivers Casino after dinner. You interested in joining us?"

Beth shrugged her shoulders, and Flora said, "Why not?"

"Great! See you in half an hour then. I'm Jim, and my friend's name is Gavin." He walked back to his table.

"Beth, I think you'll enjoy this. You can do what you want after dancing for a while–no obligation!"

"I'll go with you to the Casino, if it's not too far away, and then head back early to my hotel. I'm busted. It's been a long day, and being chased by a security guard didn't help!"

"Yeah, I saw him. They really don't like snoops around here. They're afraid of the bad publicity. Security is one of the services WOS provides to the oil companies."

After their meal they paid the waitress and ambled over to the table where Jim and Gavin were sitting. "We're ready, if you are," Flora said. She paired off with Jim, and Beth with Gavin, who was shyer.

"I'm leaving my truck here. Doesn't make sense to drive it for such a short ride," Jim said. They didn't speak much as they walked over to the Casino.

The bar was full and the dance floor crowded when they arrived. They managed to grab a table for four and ordered drinks. Beth took a sip of her margarita and put it down. It was already going to her head. *This is definitely not my night for partying*, she thought.

Gavin urged her out onto the dance floor, but after a few minutes she had enough and begged off. "Sorry guys, I'm really zonked. I've got to go back to my hotel and get some sleep. It's just a few blocks, isn't it?" After promising to get together with Flora again, she said good night and headed off on foot along Franklin Avenue.

There was no moon, and the sidewalk between the street lights seemed eerily dark. There were no other pedestrians. *This is farther than I thought. Oh well, another half kilometre and I should be there.*

A car came along on her side of the street, slowing. A guy on the passenger side rolled down his window and leered at her. "Want to have some fun?"

She looked away, and started to walk more quickly. She sighed with relief when a police cruiser turned onto Franklin from a side street. The car following her sped up and drove away. In another block she saw the sign for the Pomeroy Hotel on a street to the right. Once back in her room she crashed. She was asleep within five minutes.

8

"Hi, I'm looking for Claire Boswell," Beth told the woman at the desk just inside the Alberta Oil Sands Climate Project office. It was located in an extra-wide trailer located on a street not far from the Athabasca River, an easy walk from the Pomeroy Hotel. Though it was early Monday morning, Beth had been surprised to find that the office was already open.

The woman looked to be in her early thirties and had the lean, hungry look of an apostle for a cause. She turned to Beth. "I haven't seen her today. She may be at the Syncrude plant. There's a picket line outside their gate, waiting for the workers to arrive for the beginning of their shift. We try to hassle the assholes who desecrate the environment, so they don't forget what the rest of us think of the awful things that they do."

"When do you expect her back?"

"Hang on a sec, I'll text her. Right, she should be back in an hour or so. Want to come back then?"

Beth decided to drive to the Oil Sands Discovery Centre, which was a few kilometres south on highway 63. She learned something about their history and the methods used for mining and *in situ* extraction. *It does a good job of selling the benefits, but downplays the costs. It promises that the land will be put back to its natural state, but how credible is that?*

When she got back to the AOSCP office, Claire Boswell was at one of the desks, drafting a press release about the picket line protest. Beth saw a slender, dark haired girl in her twenties with a shy but determined expression on her face. Beth introduced herself, saying she had been given her name by an oil services company employee who had worked with her father. "Claire, tell me what's going on with the oil sands, and how you think your organization can improve things."

"You can see for yourself what the oil companies do. Their motto is: *There is no God but Moolah, and Profit is the name of the game!* They carve great swaths out of the land and inject steam into the earth, spewing out pollutants. They destroy the habitat that used to sustain my people. The main thing that needs to be done is to stop the rape of the oil sands, and that's what we're trying to do."

"How did it come to this? How were the oil companies allowed to operate here?"

"It's a long and sad story! Let me first tell you a little about my family history. My mother was a Dene whose people lived north of here, near Fort McKay. They had lived there well before the white man came to the area to hunt animals for fur, but they made peace with the newcomers and signed a treaty with the British crown in 1899. Sixty years later, extraction of petroleum from the bitumen, which is visible on the surface of the ground in many places, became economically viable. In order to get our agreement to sign over our lands to them in exchange for a share of the oil revenues, the oil companies promised the Fort McKay First Nation that they would mine the oil sands in a sustainable fashion and minimize environmental impacts. That was an outright lie, a fable told to us gullible indigenous peoples. They said we could continue to hunt and fish those lands, but what good was that right if the land was stripped of vegetation and the water was poisoned? The First Nation complained, but the oil companies and the Alberta government turned a deaf ear to our concerns.

"My father was one of the oil company workers when they started exploiting my band's ancestral lands. My parents met somehow and started dating. They argued about the rights and wrongs of the whole situation. My father started by defending the benefits from mining the bitumen, the wealth that this would produce and which would accrue to everyone. However, little by little the truth of what my mother was saying won him over. He could see first-hand the damage to the boreal forests, the loss of natural habitat for wildlife, and the deteriorating health of our people.

"After a few months, they were in sync as to the dangers from the oil sands. My parents decided to marry, though my father kept working for WOS. I was born the following year. But my mother's health was declining. She had pancreatic cancer, which I am sure was caused by consuming food and water fouled by the mining and processing of bitumen. The tailings ponds were not sealed, leeching poisons into our water and poisoning the fish. Stripping the soil to mine the oil sands exposed the game that is a main source of our food to all sorts of contaminants. My mother died when I was ten, and by that time my father was also sick, suffering from emphysema that was probably the result of the poor air quality at the mining sites. He shifted to a back office job and eventually got the company to grant him a small disability pension." Claire paused, brushing a tear away from her eye.

"Wow. So you're determined to prevent this from happening to others, but do you really think that you can shut down the oil sands?"

"Well, we've got to try to stop, or at least slow down, new development. The particle emissions from mining the oil sands are much greater than reported by the oil companies. The toxic gases include both nitrogen and sulphur oxides, which are major health risks. The *in situ* oil sands extraction method–known as Steam Assisted Gravity Drainage, or SAGD–also produces a lot of CO2 pollution. They need to superheat a lot of water to 300 degrees–five times the volume of oil that gets extracted! The process sends steam down one horizontal well to liquify the bitumen, and pumps it out from another horizontal well located below it. Making the steam uses up a lot of natural gas, but at least they recycle some of the water."

"How do you think this is going to end? The province lives on oil revenues!"

"In time, the global effort to decarbonize energy will lower the price of oil. Exploiting the oil sands will no longer be profitable. We're the high cost producers, and only conventional, low cost oil will survive at that point. It will come from places like Saudi Arabia. When that happens, of course the oil companies in Alberta won't want to remediate all the environmental damage from mining the oil sands. They'll go bankrupt and the provincial government will have to try to clean up the mining sites. The cost will be enormous–much greater than the amounts currently in the province's clean-up fund. And by that time, the government will have spent the windfall of oil revenues, which means it won't get done. So we've got to do something now to stop the environmental disaster."

"Is your father also an activist, despite having worked in the industry? How's his health?"

"He's OK for now, but he really should move somewhere else where there's less pollution. He agrees with what I do, but he's not directly involved in protesting against the oil sands–after all, one of the companies involved pays his pension, small though it is, and he doesn't want to lose it."

"They would cut off his pension just for exercising his right to free speech?"

"They could. Depends on the terms of the contract he signed when he took early retirement. In my experience, fossil fuel companies can be pretty vindictive when it comes to protests against their business. There's too much money at stake. The province backs them up."

Beth noticed graffiti on the side of the trailer. Someone had written *TRAITORS* in red paint. "Have you been attacked because you're campaigning against the oil sands?"

"Our outfit has been smeared with false accusations. Some say that we're financed by Saudi Arabia. Others claim that our head is a former Trotskyite. Both of those are lies. So far, we've faced no violence, but the provincial government threatens to take away our right to protest and does everything it can to belittle our claims."

9

Ashcroft-by-the-Sea

"**B**eth is sure taking the bit between her teeth on this commission from Jeremy Boswell," Hamish said to Sean. "She's done a lot of digging, both as regards Tom and the environment in Fort McMurray. I just hope he's satisfied with the information she's found and isn't turned off by her jumping on the ecology bandwagon."

"I told you she was a hard worker, and smart. She hasn't informed Jeremy yet about his cousin's pro-ecology positions. I'm curious what his reaction will be."

"I'll bet he's a lot more sympathetic to the oil companies and the Alberta government than Beth is. Like many Canadians with money in the stock market, he probably owns a lot of Canadian energy stocks, and most of those companies have big stakes in the oil sands." Hamish laughed. "He may be someone who's happy to stick his own head in the sand, and ignore all the damage being done there! For all I know he might even be a climate-change denier. When you're heavily invested there it's tempting to downplay the evidence on climate change in order to provide a rationale for continuing to mine the oil sands."

"That reminds me of bumper stickers I've seen on pick-up trucks that say 'I love my fossil fuels'. Even here in the Maritimes, a lot of people are invested, both literally and figuratively, in the current carbon economy."

"It's a generational thing, Sean. Many of the young people are frantic about the effects of climate change. They view as complete madness the willful ignorance of older generations with respect to environmental issues:

"The world has run amok,
The planet is out of luck.
Disaster is too mild a word;
This whole thing is just absurd.
The melting polar ice cap
Will wipe islands off the map.
It will bring tribulations
To a host of coastal populations.
The leader who denies
The truth before his eyes,
Deserves to spend his remaining days
Choking in a toxic orange haze."

"Hamish, that's a good one! Much as I hate to admit it, I think that the younger generation is probably right. We're running out of time."

*****

"So how are things out there in Fort McMurray?" Sean was on a Zoom call with Beth and Jeremy.

"I'm OK, I guess. But Oh My God, I would never have believed that the oil sands could be such an environmental disaster! Something needs to be done about it, pronto!"

Jeremy interrupted. "Ms. Phillips, could we turn to what I am paying you to look into, namely the activities of my cousin Tom Boswell? How is he? What has been doing for the last thirty or so years?"

"As I reported to you earlier, Mr. Boswell, he's been working for an oil services outfit, and is now retired on a disability pension. As far as I know, he doesn't do much now, though his daughter is all in with an environmental advocacy group, the Alberta Oil Sands Climate Project. Her mother, a Dene who grew up in Fort McKay, died young of cancer that was probably brought on by exposure to toxins from the oil sands."

"That's a serious allegation. Can she prove it?"

"Probably not. Health services are pretty rudimentary on the reserve."

"In any case, the oil sands have always been there, and may have fouled the air and water even before oil extraction started. So you can't necessarily lay the blame on the oil companies."

"Yeah, sure, that's the alibi the oil companies and the Alberta government peddle. It's bullshit."

Sean stepped in. "The question we need to decide is what we should do now. Mr. Boswell, is there anything else Beth should try to find out in Fort McMurray, or is she done? And are there other things Hamish and I can look into for you?"

"I think the time has come for me to go out to Alberta to see my cousin. Beth, if you would stay there until I arrive, you can help set things up. In the meantime, would you meet again with Tom and explain the situation, without promising any legacy? Just tell him that I would like to talk to him. Unless he objects, I'll be coming as soon as I can make the travel arrangements. Is that satisfactory?"

"Yes, boss. Whatever you say. Do you want to meet with his daughter as well? If so, I'll make sure she knows you're coming and arrange for the three of you to get together."

"Yes, go ahead. Just don't get involved with the movement protesting the oil sands!"

When Jeremy got off the call, Sean continued the conversation with Beth. "I'd like to join you out there, but the case I'm working on is reaching a critical point. You know, the thefts at Andy's boat yard? Something's got to be done. He's climbing the walls! Hopefully I can get a lead and track down who's involved. If I do, I can come out to visit you in Alberta. I'll let you know."

10

"This is the third time someone has had his outboard motor stolen–in this case Jim Thompson had his old Grady White with a new Yamaha 150 taken from its slip," Andy told Sean angrily. Andy was only a few years younger than Sean, but his round face and shock of blond hair made him look like a well-worn teenager. "He just had the engine installed two months ago on his boat, and it cost him over 30 thousand all told! And now his insurance company is refusing to pay, claiming that it's my fault! They say that three thefts prove that the marina is negligent. Even if they do pay off in the end, they probably won't renew his coverage. If insurance companies do the same for the others who keep their boats here, I'll lose all my customers. They'll move their boats to other marinas where they can get insurance. My marina will go bust."

"Andy, I sincerely sympathize and understand what you feel. I'll do my best, but as I told you when I took the job, this is a tough case, and I offer no guarantees."

"Sure, sure, but get your ass in gear! If I have to hire a night watchman, I'll do it. After the first theft occurred on your advice I installed security cameras but the video doesn't show us squat! We can't afford to have another theft. If we do, I'll be out of business!"

"Wasn't the engine locked? How did they manage to get the boat out of the marina?"

"Of course it was locked, and a steel cable attached the boat to a ring bolt on the dock! But the bastards had cable cutters, and they probably jimmied the engine lock since the videos don't show the boat being towed out of the marina."

"I'll want to look over the surveillance videos. How much do you think they can get for the boat and motor?"

"I'll bet they can easily get $10k for the motor. A lot less than it's worth, but still a nice little windfall. You need to locate ads for used engines and look at the engines themselves to compare their serial numbers with Jim's. The thieves may scuttle the hull itself since it's old and too easily identified."

"He's reported the theft to the police. They should be looking around for a Grady White and that model Yamaha engine for sale."

"They should, but they're not. They're too busy, they say. If someone reports a suspicious sale–say a price that's too good to be true–then they'll investigate. But they don't have the manpower to search the boating equipment ads online. Anyway, it could be that the thieves just put a note with an advert on some marina's bulletin board so you'd have to go around to local marinas to find it. They're not going to do it, so it's up to us."

"OK, I can do that. But first I'd like to look over the footage from the security cameras."

"I tell you, there's nothing suspicious there. That's the weird thing! The boat can't have disappeared into thin air!"

Andy took Sean to his office and showed him how to access the recordings. "Just log on to the security company's website using my user id and password and you can look at the videos taken by the cameras installed at the marina. They stream the video via WiFi to the security company. After a week, the recordings are erased from the server."

Sean left the marina, which was only a few kilometres from The Oaks, and drove back home. He sat in front of the desktop in the detective agency's office with a cup of coffee and settled in for a long session scrolling through the surveillance videos. The latest theft had occurred sometime during the night, so he started the video at dusk the day before. He displayed synchronized feeds from three of the cameras on a split screen: one showing the boat, *Ms. B. Haven*, whose motor was stolen, at its dock; another displaying the channel that led into the marina from the bay; and a third showing the front entrance to the marina as seen from the road. The boatyard was accessed through a sliding gate that required a magnetic card to enter, but when a vehicle approached it from the inside it opened automatically. There was also a pedestrian gate which was opened by entering a code on a keypad.

At first, a few boat owners who had been working on their boats were seen leaving the boatyard by the vehicle gate. Then there was a long period of inactivity. Sean assumed that the marina was now empty of people but was surprised to see someone entering the marina's washroom, which was close to the front gate. He made a note to ask Andy whether the marina allowed liveaboards. It was usually OK at most marinas for an owner to spend the night aboard his or her boat occasionally, for instance when leaving on an early cruise the next morning.

The video feed that gave a view of *Ms. B. Haven* did not show anyone approaching or leaving the boat, which was tied up to the dock on its starboard side.

After 11 pm there was no further visible activity on any of the three screens until just before sunrise, aside from the visit of the occasional Canada goose or neighbourhood cat. At 5 am the vehicle gate opened to admit the first of a number of fishermen who motored out in their boats a little while later. Andy's was a favourite marina for fishermen, since it was the nearest to the bay, which was reputed as a fishing ground. He counted a dozen boats leaving the marina.

Sean called Andy's cell. "I haven't seen anything suspicious. You haven't kept any of the videos made around the time of the second boat theft?"

"I did. I downloaded them to my computer, so when they were deleted on the server I could still look at them. I'll forward them to you. I should warn you that I didn't see anything suspicious. But it doesn't hurt to have another pair of eyes look them over."

"Oh, and another thing: do you allow liveaboards?"

"No, the marina contract forbids anyone to spend more than three consecutive nights aboard at the dock. Less than that is OK, and I know that some people with bigger boats do it frequently, most every weekend. But they don't have to ask permission so I don't know who's aboard at any given time. I'll bet it's mostly those who have sailboats, since they're the ones with comfortable living quarters, not the fishing boats."

11

Sean looked over the CCTV feeds for the second boat theft, with an outboard motor of similar horsepower as the Yamaha, but a different make–a Mercury. It would be easy to sell the engine separately, as many boaters would be attracted by a bargain price, and this was a popular size.

The footage largely told the same story as for the third theft, namely little visible overnight activity and the arrival, in the early morning, of fishermen who motored away at daybreak. No one could be seen approaching the boat at its dock during the night, though the surveillance video did not give a complete view of the runabout.

Sean, discouraged, was about to give up when he scrolled back to the hour before dawn and counted the number of fishermen who drove into the marina. Then he scrolled forward to count the boats that motored away. There was one more of the latter than of the former. He returned to the video of the third theft. The same was true there. Sean exulted. *Aha! I wonder if someone spent the night at the marina, getting onto the boat without being seen, and left, pretending to be one of the fishermen.*

Andy, when told, looked through the videos again. "Sonofabitch, I see what you mean. But shit, I can't identify all those who came in through the gate that morning on the video, or who's on the boats leaving the marina. It's too dark. So we still don't have a clue who pirated the boats. It's back to square one."

"Wouldn't the other fishermen have had a good look at the boat going out, and realized that it was being operated by someone who wasn't its owner?"

"Not necessarily. It was still dark, and it would be easy for the pirate to wear a hoodie to avoid being ID'd. Anyway, the fishermen don't pal around much. They don't want to reveal their favourite fishing spots."

12

Sean called Andy with a plan. "I think the best way to catch your thieves–assuming the three boats were stolen by the same gang–would be to have someone spend the night at your marina. Not necessarily a night watchman. If you hire someone and stick him in the office, you may simply scare away the thief. So my plan would be to dock my sailboat here, and pretend I'm just a transient boater renting a slip for a day or two. I can watch what's going on. What do you think?"

"It might work. But unless you plan to stay here for a long time, what are your chances of being on the spot just the night they do their dirty work?"

"I've looked at the dates of the three thefts, and they're all on a Friday night into Saturday, two weeks apart. So the guys involved obviously have a weekday occupation. And the last theft was 10 days ago. So if I sail here this coming Friday, I might just be in luck."

"OK, let's give it a shot."

*****

Sean had bought a used Canadian Sailcraft CS 30 sailboat, named *Spray* after the first boat to be sailed around the world single-handed–by Joshua Slocum in the late 19th century. Sean had so far cruised the boat along Nova Scotia's South Shore and captained her at the Ashcroft Yacht Club's Wednesday night races. Beth was starting to enjoy going out sailing with him, but since she was in Alberta at present, Sean sailed alone from AYC to Andy's Marina. Friday afternoon was as nice a summer day as he could hope for, bright sunshine, though coolish on the water. Coming into the marina, he carefully steered well off the breakwater to avoid the rocks before easing into the entrance channel and tying up at the slip that Andy had assigned to him.

The marina was busy, as was often the case at the beginning of the weekend. Transient boaters who had sailed down from Halifax or over from the States hailed the marina on VHF channel 16 asking for a slip assignment–most of them having made an advance reservation. A large Irwin sailboat with a US registration pulled into the slip next to Sean's boat. Sean, seeing it coming, got onto the dock to help them tie up. It was sailed by a couple who were about Sean's age, the husband at the wheel and the wife on deck holding a dock line in preparation for jumping off. She looked worried. Sean grabbed the boat's lifelines and prevented the vessel from being blown away from its dock by the crosswind, allowing the woman to disembark safely and tie off the bow and stern lines.

The couple thanked Sean profusely, who replied "No problem," thinking, *It's a good thing I was here, otherwise the Irwin might have damaged the side of my boat, given all the windage it has!* "Where are you from?" he asked.

"We keep our boat in Bar Harbor, Maine. This is our first cruise away from home!"

"Nice. I think you'll enjoy it here." He hoped that the newbies would avoid any serious mishaps. *Boating opens up your life to a whole range of new experiences: some good, some bad; all of them expensive!*

Sean walked along the other docks to stretch his legs. The bigger sailboats, with their deeper draughts, were moored near the entrance to the marina. Most of the small power boats were in the inner slips, which were both shallower and narrower. There was a bait table there, which was also used for cleaning fish. A few gulls circled expectantly overhead, hoping for their next meal. He noted that most of the slips here were occupied, though no one was on the boats. *Probably the fishermen came back from their early morning outings hours ago, and have gone home.*

Sean went back to *Spray* and lay down in the v-berth for a nap. *I plan to be up much of the night. Better get some rest while I can.*

At six p.m. he awoke and prepared himself a pasta dinner on the boat's propane stove. The marina was quieter now. Many of the transients had wandered off to the shopping mall that was a few hundred metres away. It housed a McDonalds and a restaurant that served mainly fish and chips. Sean checked out access to the marina. The parking lot required a magnetic card to get in. A locked gate provided access to the docks. Seasonal slip holders and transient visitors were provided with a four-digit access code. *I don't think this gets changed very often, so any number of people might have the code.*

It being Friday evening there was still a fairly noisy group of boaters celebrating the end of the week. As it began to get dark some of the locals returned home while others retreated to the cabins of their boats. The marina became quiet, and Sean was one of the few still on deck. He kept *Spray's* deck lights off in order better to observe what might be going on around him. Nothing much was happening, and he dozed off.

He awoke with a crick in his neck from leaning back against the coaming. His cellphone told him that it was just after midnight. He heard a faint whirring noise. *That must have woken me,* he thought. *I wonder what it is.*

Not being able to locate exactly where the noise was coming from, he swivelled around, staring into the darkness. There was nothing visible on the docks, which were lit by pedestal lights at five metre intervals. The darkness on the water below the docks, however, was impenetrable.

The noise was still very faint, and Sean had convinced himself that it must be due to a water pump or air conditioner on some boat, when he heard a louder splash. It was clearly coming from the inner docks where the powerboats were tied up. Sean crept out of the cockpit onto his dock. Wearing dark clothing and soft soled shoes, he tried to avoid the lighted areas as he made his way toward the place from which the noise had come.

Seeing some movement on one of the boats tied up to a dock parallel to the one where he was walking, he ducked down behind a trawler with a large navigation station which gave him some cover. He observed a shadowy figure slipping over the gunwale of the boat into its cockpit. Another shape in a small boat on the water passed some object to the first one. Sean could see that they had boarded a centre console boat with a cabin, and that the two individuals were working at opening the hatch that led into it.

Sean hesitated. He could not see attempting to thwart the two thieves alone, especially since they might be armed. He crept back to his own boat and hid in his cabin, putting the companionway boards back in place. Without turning on cabin lights, he called Andy on his cellphone. "I think we have thieves at work trying to hijack another boat. They're on the centre console boat in slip A-10. I'm guessing that they're going to lie low in its cabin until first light, then leave with the fishermen."

"That's Bud Reagan's boat. They must know that he isn't using it much, so he's not likely to surprise them on his boat before they can get it out of the marina. Keep an eye on them if you can. I'll call the police."

Sean got out his night-vision binoculars and focused on slip A-10. No one was on deck, but he could see a faint glimmer of light coming from one of the boat's ports. Then it went out. *I guess they're settling in for the night. I'll check on them later. In the meantime, I'll get a little shut-eye.*

The vibration of his cellphone woke him up. It was 4 am. "Sean, this is Andy. The RCMP says that they can't come before morning unless it's an emergency. So it's up to us. I'm coming over. I'll try to sneak into the marina without making too much noise. Soon the fishermen will be coming in too, and our thieves will be on their way. We've got to stop the bastards!"

Sean opened the hatch and crept into the cockpit. *Still no one visible on deck on the centre console.* He looked at the entrance to the marina and spotted a figure stealthily opening the gate that led to the docks and heading his way. He waited until Andy came alongside the dock where *Spray* was tied up. Motioning to him to be quiet, he whispered, "Let's go below, they're less likely to hear us."

"Sean, our best bet to stop them would be to disable their engine so they can't get out of the marina. Then we can hope that the RCMP can get here in time to nab them."

"You think they've been able to jimmy the engine lock? I didn't see anyone working on it. They'd be visible at the stern. Besides, they would have to grind off the lock, making a lot of noise."

"OK then, how do they get the boat out of the marina?"

A gentle whirring noise came from that direction. Sean grabbed his binoculars. "They're moving! They can't have started the engine or we would have heard them! It must be an electric trolling motor." Sean turned the key to start his own diesel inboard engine, put it in gear, and quickly headed for the entrance channel. The centre console was moving slowly but steadily. It had a head start, but its dock was farther from the channel than *Spray's*.

Sean pushed the throttle to its maximum, revving the engine to 3000 rpm. The boat careened past other docked boats, paralleling the centre console which was two docks over. The channels converged at the entrance that opened onto the bay. Narrowly preceding the centre console, Sean turned sharply to the right and slammed the gear lever into reverse. The sailboat slowed down and stopped athwart the channel entrance, blocking passage by the centre console.

"Look out, she's going to hit us!" At the last second, the powerboat veered to starboard, attempting to find a narrow path between the stern of the sailboat and the breakwater. It narrowly missed *Spray* and seemed to have succeeded in escaping. Then the boat made a screeching sound as a submerged rock tore a strip out of its fibreglass hull. It continued moving forward for a few seconds, then started settling into the water. It was clear that the boat would not be able to go much further. The man steering the boat left the helm and clambered onto the side deck. He and the other man on board hesitated a moment, then jumped off onto the rocks of the breakwater, leaving the boat adrift.

Andy grabbed the bow of the sinking powerboat with a boat hook. "We've got to save Bud's pride and joy! Can you tow it to the boat launch? It'll rest on its keel in the shallow water of the ramp, preventing it from sinking. Then we should then be able to get her on a trailer." Andy quickly grabbed a dock line that was attached to *Spray's* stern, gingerly stepping onto the powerboat and tying the line to a cleat at its bow. "Go, go! It's sinking fast!"

Sean gunned the engine of his sailboat again in forward gear and raced toward the boat launch. When only 10 metres away he shouted to Andy, "Cast off your bow line!" before veering sharply to port and shifting into reverse to slow his boat down.

The powerboat's momentum allowed it to glide toward the launch ramp, coming to rest on the bottom in two feet of water. Sean tied up his sailboat at a nearby vacant dock, then came over to help secure the centre console.

Only then did they notice in the dawning light that the two thieves had succeeded in crawling up the rocks of the break-water and onto a path that led back to the marina office. Now they were running toward the entrance to the marina. Andy and Sean were too far away to catch them, but some fishermen were arriving at the front gate. Andy shouted: "Stop them!" while pointing at the fugitives. A pair of burly men in camo suits looked in the direction Andy had pointed. Realizing what he meant, they blocked the doorway. When the thieves tried to force their way past, the fishermen tackled them and held them down on the ground while Sean and Andy made their way there. Andy retrieved some plastic zip ties from the office and Sean used them to attach their wrists and ankles. Andy called the RCMP again. "You can come and pick up the thieves. We've got 'em."

"Sean, they should be here in about half an hour." Andy turned to examine the two men they had captured.

"Hey, I recognize you!" he said to the elder of the two, a slender man in his forties wearing grease-stained jeans and a dark windbreaker. "You used to have a boat here. I guess that's how you know so much about this place! You figured out which boats don't get used much, so you thought you could get on them without getting caught." The man looked at the ground, a snarl on his lips, saying nothing. The other man also stayed silent. He appeared to be in his early twenties, and might have been his son. His face showed dismay at the prospect of spending his young adulthood in prison.

Sean said to Andy, "I figured out why they made so little noise. They must have brought the trolling motor with them so they didn't have to work on the outboard engine's lock. That would make a hell of a racket. Those electric trolling motors with a lithium battery are so light they can easily be carried in a kayak. And the fishermen seeing them go out wouldn't find navigating with a trolling motor suspicious, since they all use them. There was a two-man inflatable kayak inside the centre console. That's how they got into the marina undetected. And no one would see it after it was deflated and stowed away."

Andy turned to one of the two men who had tackled the thieves. "Charlie, you sure got here just in time to catch those sonsabitches! Tell you what, when we're done with the police I'll buy you both breakfast at McDonald's."

"Sure Andy, happy to do our bit. This is my brother Ross. I don't think we'll be doing any fishing today anyhow."

After half an hour a police cruiser arrived. A detective took Sean and Andy's testimonies, as well as those of Charlie and Ross, while a constable put cuffs on the thieves and locked them in the back of the cruiser.

"Make sure you look for any evidence that they also did the other boat thefts," Andy told the RCMP agents as they prepared to drive back to their detachment office. "We're still short a couple of boats and their outboard engines."

Sean explained how he happened to be there, and what he had observed before the final showdown with the boat thieves. "I'll be happy to make a statement. Please give my regards to Joe Washington. He's got my contact details." Joe had been his classmate at Riverview High School several decades before. He now headed the Lunenburg Detachment of the RCMP.

After the RCMP agents had left with their prisoners, Andy turned to Sean with a sigh of relief. "This has turned out a lot better than I feared. We caught the thieves and saved one of the boats. If it had sunk, the salt water would've buggered the engine in short order. Bud Reagan's gonna be proud of us. Anyway, what we've done should get the insurance companies off my back!"

"Andy. I think I've done the job that you hired me to do. I'm going to head out to Alberta. Beth's out there and since she's new to the detective business, I want to make sure that she's doing what she's supposed to. Are you OK with that?"

"Sure, Sean. You did good!"

*****

But when Sean called Beth, she was reluctant for him to come. "I'm almost done here. I'm just waiting for Jeremy to come and talk to Tom and Claire. You'd just get in the way, and it would be a trip for nothing. Anyway, I should be home soon."

13

Fort McMurray

Beth, Tom Boswell and his daughter Claire were sitting at a table in the Keg Steakhouse in downtown Fort McMurray. Beth explained why she had invited them. "I was spoofing you when I talked to you earlier, both of you. I was hired to locate you, Tom, by your cousin Jeremy Boswell. He'd like to meet with you again, after all these years. For what purpose, he didn't say. But I think it's for some sort of reconciliation."

"What? Jeremy wants to get in touch! That's unbelievable!"

"Yes, he explained to me that he's been haunted by what happened to his girlfriend decades ago in Orangedale, Nova Scotia."

"Oh, so you know that the last time we saw each other was over the dead body of a girl both of us were in love with, or thought we were. And her death was our fault."

"Yes, he filled me in on the sad story, Tom."

Claire's face was ravaged by the news she had heard. "You never told me about this, Dad! What happened?"

67

"I've tried to forget that day ever since, and I don't want to talk about it. Let's just say if I'd known the train accident was going to happen, I'd have acted differently. But the past can't be undone."

"So this cousin was there too?"

"Yes, Claire, I think Margaret was especially trying to save him, not me, when she fell on the tracks in front of the speeding train. He was her favourite. He probably still blames me for what happened, and hates me for it. Did he tell you why he wants to see me? Is he going to exact his revenge?"

"Jeremy said he just wanted to re-engage with you. In any case, he's coming as soon as he can from Halifax, unless you'd rather not see him. I can understand if you'd prefer not."

"No, let him come. It'll be good to see family after all these years, since there's nobody else left. I don't know if we'll hit it off. We'll see."

"So, what are your plans for the future, now that you're retired? Are you going to join Claire in organizing protests against exploitation of the oil sands?"

He laughed. "I might take up golf. That or fishing along the Athabasca River."

"Dad, those things are only possible for a few months out of the year, and I sure wouldn't want to eat the fish caught in that river! You really should try to find a place to live that has a milder climate and less pollution, like Arizona! Your emphysema will just get worse and worse."

"Yeah, yeah, I hear you. But unless I win the lottery I'm stuck here. Besides, I want to be near you." He pinched her cheek.

*****

Beth and Tom Boswell met Jeremy at the Fort McMurray airport at the end of the afternoon. There were only a dozen or so passengers on the Air Canada flight so spotting him was not difficult. They waved, Tom saying to Beth, "I would never have recognized him on the street after so many years. Age gets to all of us, doesn't it?"

Driving back to the Pomeroy Hotel in Beth's rental car, conversation was subdued. Jeremy said he was tired after his trip from Halifax, which had taken most of the day, given stops in Toronto and Calgary. "Let me have a little rest. Then can I invite you to join me for dinner?"

Beth nodded, and Tom said, "I'd love to. Can I suggest Zembaba, a Somali restaurant? It's only a short walk from the hotel, and the food's quite good."

"Sure, let's give it a try. Could we all meet in the lobby of the hotel in an hour? You can show me the way to the restaurant."

"Any objection if we include my daughter Claire?" Tom added.

"No, not at all. I'm looking forward to meeting her."

*****

"I gather, Tom, that you've been living in Fort McMurray for the past twenty-odd years? What's that like?" Jeremy was making conversation while sipping a beer, as the four of them sat at a table at Zembaba and waited for their food.

"OK, I guess, though as Claire will tell you it's discouraging to see what exploiting the oil sands has done to the natural environment. We had to evacuate when the wildfires destroyed much of the town a few years back. I went to live in Edmonton for two months, where Claire was going to university. When I returned, my house was nothing but ashes. It was a long slog making Fort McMurray liveable again. This year, a wildfire approached the town and forced evacuations. And yet once again the oil companies are mining as much oil from the oil sands as they can, adding to the global warming that is helping fuel the fires."

Jeremy bristled. "Now wait a minute there! You can't blame the oil sands for the 2016 fire! It was a once in a lifetime event!"

Claire jumped in. "What started the fire hasn't been discovered, though it's thought to be some human activity. But what made the fire so devastating was the dryness of the forests and high temperatures–and that was caused by global warming."

"So you say. Others disagree."

Claire said angrily, "Surely you can't deny that Alberta is taking the wrong path! The scientific evidence shows that CO2 levels are rising continuously and each year we experience record heat. Despite that, the provincial government is discouraging development of renewables, such as solar and wind, to show its support for the oil sands! And the regulatory authority greenwashes all the environmental effects of oil extraction. We're driving over a cliff, and those who are making money doing it don't give a fuck."

Jeremy became animated. "Canada has to exploit its comparative advantage in oil and gas. The world is going to have to continue to use those fuels, and we've got a massive amount of reserves. It's a pipe dream to think we can convert everything to electricity and generate all of it by wind and solar!"

Tom intervened. "OK, maybe not, but there's also nuclear and hydro. The sooner we get serious about moving away from fossil fuels, the better off we'll be. What's the point of killing ourselves with pollution from the oil sands just to make money?"

"It's going to take decades. So in the meantime, we should develop secure sources of domestic oil, rather than be dependent on foreign energy. And we can decrease our carbon footprint by carbon capture and storage."

Claire clenched her fists, and her face had turned red. "By shutting down the oil sands, we could massively cut back on energy use! Fully a third of the natural gas burned in Canada goes to heat the water for *in situ* extraction of bitumen from the oil sands and upgrading. So we're compounding the negative effects of fossil fuels on global warming! And as for carbon capture, it's a mirage conjured up by the industry to allow it to continue on its merry way pumping CO2 into the atmosphere!"

Jeremy stood up. "I don't want to listen to this any more from you two, and I know you've also got Beth on your side. It was a mistake to come here. I wanted to see relatives, and was thinking of including you in my will, but now I've heard enough. I'm not going to leave my money to a bunch of tree-hugging bleeding-heart fanatics! Tom, you're as wrong-headed now as you were when you were a teenager, and Claire is even worse!" He waved the waiter away. "I don't want that food. Good night!" He stalked out, leaving the three of them to eat their dinners and pay the bill.

*****

Beth let Jeremy alone to think about things before speaking to him again. *Maybe he'll feel better after he gets a good night's sleep.* The next day, however, he was as angry as the night before.

"Would you book me a return flight to Halifax? I want to get out of here as soon as possible. And I'm going to be complaining to Hamish Cameron about this! You've turned my attempt to reconnect with my relatives into a fiasco."

Beth didn't see any more of him until it was time for him to catch his flight in the afternoon. She assumed that he had gone for a walk, since he didn't answer her call to his room. *Or maybe he's gone to see his pals at Wildcat Oil Services,* she thought. *They deserve each other.*

Beth and Jeremy didn't speak during the drive to the airport in her rental car. She pulled up to the departures drop off and waited for him to get out. Jeremy grabbed his bag from the back seat and strode to the check-in counter without saying goodbye. In a few minutes he was on the plane, waiting to begin his journey back to Halifax.

14

Victoria

Hamish picked Izzie up at her flat near Dalhousie University, and they drove to Halifax's Stanfield Airport to catch their flight to Toronto, and thence to Victoria. Izzie had a carry-on bag and a briefcase with notes for the talk she was going to give at the conference on securities law. "This should be fun. A day with my colleagues, then we can do the tourist thing, visiting the gardens and walking along the seashore. What do you want to do?"

"I'm going to sample some of the downtown museums and art galleries while you're working–if you can call that work!" He grinned at her.

"Well, you know that it's useful to schmooze with colleagues, find out what they're working on and what interesting issues have come up. We don't work in a vacuum, you know. Even with the Internet, face-to-face communication is still important."

It was early evening when they finally landed at Victoria airport, which was actually in Sidney. They took a cab to the

Hotel Grand Pacific, near to the Victoria Conference Centre. Since it was after midnight, Atlantic time, they crashed as soon as they made it to their room.

The next morning Hamish and Izzie went for a walk after an early breakfast. "My first session doesn't start until 10, so I have plenty of time to get over there and register," Izzie pointed out. They strolled the docks down to Fisherman's Wharf and back, Hamish going back to the hotel while Izzie proceeded to the conference centre.

Hamish wandered into various galleries that were testimony to Victoria's vibrant arts community. *It must be the magnificent scenery of the Pacific Northwest that attracts artists here, and inspires them to paint the soaring mountains, majestic trees, and wooded islands floating on an endless sea*, he thought. *Victoria itself is such a civilized place. Who would not want to live close to nature while enjoying the warmth of human companionship here?*

Hamish had been back at the hotel for half an hour when Izzie returned. "I had an interesting day. My talk on cryptocurrency securities went well, I thought. It stimulated a lot of discussion. I said that crypto was yet another financial innovation that has created opportunities for fleecing the public. Its complications baffle the unwary and lure them into scams. Crypto's main use is to avoid government regulation, so it's a natural conduit for money laundering. Otherwise, it's a solution to a non-existent problem. If you want a good store of value, a currency that is stable, who should you put your faith in, someone you don't know who creates a new form of money that is backed by nothing, or an established central bank with a good track record that is backed by the taxing power of the government? As for crypto denominated securities, they're likely to be issued only by high risk borrowers who have trouble raising money elsewhere. Making the principal fluctuate with the value of some dubious currency just adds a layer of risk to the asset. When the bubble caused by the current fascination with crypto bursts, lenders are going to lose their shirts."

"I can see you don't have anything good to say about crypto!"

"The distributed ledger is an interesting innovation, but not the currency itself. Besides, do we really want to waste enormous amounts of electricity to do the mining needed to create crypto?"

"OK, let's leave it there and decide on where to go for dinner!"

They settled on an Italian restaurant near the harbour that was only a short walk away. The traditional dishes were excellently prepared, and they shared a nice Barolo. After a few glasses, they reminisced about their relationship over the years.

"I'm glad we never got married," Izzie said. "We probably wouldn't be friends now if we had."

"Oh, why so?"

"You've gotten more irascible over the years, and I've become more focussed on my work. Neither is good for a relationship. And when a married couple gets old, they have to spend most of their time together because they have fewer outside activities."

"That's true. And being too similar in character is also bad, because it makes a relationship too brittle. As we change with age, we may well become less alike, which puts stress on a marriage. An initially like-minded couple is not set up to handle that. In contrast, if you're attracted to your partner from the start because he or she is different, then you can adapt to other differences that develop later. We started out as lawyers, with the same interests and profession. Now you're a professor, and I'm a gumshoe. I don't think you'd like living with a detective."

Izzie nodded her head in agreement. "I'm also happy not to have had children–not that being married is necessary for that. But when you think of it, another child in the world is adding another being with the carbon footprint of a herd of elephants! The infant needs to be fed, clothed, housed with central heating and cooling, and when it matures it will want to have its own car and travel around the world by plane, train, cruise ship, or other forms of transportation that burns fossil fuels. The only way we as a species can survive given our current habits is to shrink the population. That's my view, anyway."

"What a cheery thought! You were always someone who didn't shy away from hard truths."

As they were debating whether their food debauchery should extend to dessert, Hamish noticed a familiar face on a solo diner who had just been seated. Hamish said, "That's someone I used to know in law school, Francis Lee. Last I heard, he was a member of the BC Legislative Assembly. I'll say hello to him on the way out."

After some chocolate mousse and a glass of port–a shared single serving of each–they were ready to leave. Hamish went round to his friend's table. "Hello Francis, it's been a long time! How are you? I heard you were an MLA here in BC. Are you still doing that?"

The other man looked up quizzically, then nodded and smiled. "Hamish, what a surprise! Yes, I'm still an MLA, though maybe not for long. And what brings you to Vancouver Island?"

"My friend Izzie French is here for a conference on securities regulation. I thought I would come along for the ride. We're planning on doing tourist stuff tomorrow."

Izzie shook his hand and said, "Pleased to meet you."

Turning back to Hamish, Francis Lee said, "You used to be a judge in Nova Scotia. Are you retired?"

"That's right, mandatory retirement at 75. I'm actually a partner in a detective agency now. What about you; are you planning to hang up your skates? Is that why you said you wouldn't be an MLA for much longer?"

"No, it's more complicated than that. I'm being targeted by another political party for my stance on fossil fuels and by the Chinese government for my criticism of their human rights record. Twenty percent of the population in my riding has some Chinese heritage, and China is doing its best to turn them against me."

"That's too bad. What are you going to do about it? Have you reported this foreign political interference to the RCMP?"

"What can I do? I'm at wit's end. I don't have any proof, just suspicions. I think it's being orchestrated by the opposition because of my stance on oil and gas exports, unsuccessful though my efforts have been. I tried but failed to stop the expansion of the Trans Mountain Pipeline. If there's a shipping accident involving a tanker from the Westridge Marine Terminal it will be catastrophic for Vancouver and surrounding areas. Not to mention the damage to the environment from the extraction, processing, and use of petroleum from the oil sands. I was also against the construction of the CoastalGasLink from the Montney Formation to the northern BC LNG terminal, but failed to stop it. Nevertheless, I'll continue to voice my opposition to more pipelines and LNG exports."

"It sounds like you have a lot of enemies. What do you have against LNG?"

"It's just wrong to tout LNG as the clean fuel that's going to replace dirty coal in the rest of the world and limit global warming. Natural gas contains a lot of methane, which is an even worse greenhouse gas than CO2. There are plenty of opportunities for leakage during extracting, liquifying, and transporting the natural gas, and methane will do a lot of damage to the environment. That's in addition to the quantity of CO2 spilling into the atmosphere when you burn the gas."

"OK, I see that the oil and gas sector wants your skin. If by any chance you need the help of a private investigator, let me know. Here's my card."

Hamish and Izzie bade him goodnight and walked back to their hotel, cooled by the pleasant breeze blowing in from the ocean. "What a beautiful evening," Izzie murmured, as she snuggled up to Hamish.

15

Ashcroft-by-the-Sea

The RCMP cruiser, driven by a uniformed constable, parked in The Oaks' driveway. Joe Washington got out, and rang the front door bell. When Sean opened the door, Joe said, "I thought I would stop by to fill you in on our investigation of the boat thefts. Can I come in for a minute or two?" The constable stayed outside near the car.

"The two thieves we caught with your help don't seem to be the whole gang. We searched their house–incidentally, the young guy is the son, and he lives at home–but didn't find any trace of the other boats or anything that pointed to their involvement in the earlier thefts. We found something puzzling on the boat they stole, though. It was a printout of information about the boat's gear, its location, and the address of its owner, Bud Reagan, downloaded from outboards.com. It's not clear why Bud would have kept it on the boat, or whether it was brought there by the thieves. In any case, they have a lawyer who's told them not to talk. If they did, they might tell us who they work for. So we're at a dead end."

"You think they're part of a larger gang, and the earlier thefts were done by others in the gang?"

"That's what we think, but we have no proof of it yet."

"The best bet would be to locate the boats and engines stolen earlier, and trace them back to someone trying to sell them."

"Unfortunately, we don't have the manpower, nor, frankly, the expertise with boats to do that."

"So who does? What about the Coast Guard?"

"They do, but they have too many operational responsibilities to get involved with investigating the thefts of pleasure boats. They're more concerned with safety on the water, smuggling, and illegal immigration. So, can you continue what you started by doing, Sean, and try to track down the stolen engines? We need you to poke around various marinas and look for boats and engines for sale that match those that were stolen. We can do the heavy lifting but you would have to identify the suspects."

"And who would pay Cameron and Carroll for this? Andy has no further need for my services. "

"I'll bet that the companies that insured the boats would want to hire you."

Sean shrugged his shoulders. "I guess I could talk to them. But I don't promise anything. Anyway, I'll let you know."

Joe slapped him on the back. "OK, that's my guy."

Sean looked at him with a grim smile. "Our collaboration hasn't worked out that well in the past. We do the work, and you take the credit!"

"Yeah, yeah, I know. But we got pressure from the higher-ups to show some wins. Our stock with the public isn't very high these days, especially in Nova Scotia."

*****

The claims adjuster for small boat insurance was enthusiastic. "Yes, we can hire you to continue investigating these thefts. I've been in contact with the RCMP, and they assure me that you're the one who's most knowledgeable about them. We'll pay our usual terms, plus expenses, for 30 days, with the possibility of renewal."

Sean proceeded to search online sites that advertised boats and motors in Nova Scotia, including Kijiji, boatsalesby-owner.com, etc. Nothing popped up as an obvious match. *I'm going to have to keep going around to individual marinas,* he thought. *Maybe also the yacht brokers, though I suspect a thief would stay away from them because they're too savvy. They would ask for documentation and spot a scam.*

Sean stopped at a marina in Chester, and looked at their notice board. There were no motors or boats that corresponded to any of the thefts at Andy's. His route took him past a yacht broker whom he knew, so he stopped to have a chat. He found Sam in his office, doing some paperwork on a motor yacht he was listing on his website.

Sam, who was a jovial middle-aged man with a bit of a paunch, greeted him warmly. "I'll be happy to sell you a yacht, Sean. I assume you've finally seen the light and are abandoning sail for power boats?"

"Ha, ha! No, I'm investigating those boat thefts over at Andy's Marina. Have you heard anything about them? Any thoughts about who might have done 'em?"

"Nope, but I did hear something interesting from an American broker located in Maine I sometimes do business with. He said some stolen Canadian outboard engines were being offered for sale down there. He doesn't have any proof but that's the rumour. He's very careful to check serial numbers before dealing with used engines."

"Interesting. So the gang that's doing the thefts up here might be smuggling them across the border. How would they do that?"

"I'm guessing they might just be putting an extra engine on the back of their boat. You know that now it's not unusual to see, for instance, a Gamefisherman with 3 engines–250 or 300 hp each–on the stern. It's crazy the amount of power you've got, and you can cruise along at 40-50 knots! You don't need that! Anyway, it would be easy to clear into the States, leave one of the engines there, and then return to Canada. They would need confederates down there, of course, so it would have to be a pretty sophisticated operation. But that's my bet."

"Probably US custom agents wouldn't require serial numbers of the engines on a visiting Canadian boat, and when returning the CBSA wouldn't have a record of how many engines the boat had when it left Canada. The problem would be selling the engines in the States."

16

Vancouver

"Hamish, this is Francis Lee. You left me your card the other day at the restaurant, and told me to call if I needed your services. And I do!"

Hamish and Izzie had just got back to their hotel room in Victoria after visiting Butchart Gardens. "Tell me what's the matter, Francis. You sound frantic."

"I am! I've just been charged with electoral fraud, because of receiving out-of-province donations, which is illegal in BC. The money I received came from a company I'd never heard of, Wildcat Oil Services, and I had no idea it came from Alberta, but that's what they say now. And, in addition, the RCMP allege that I'm an agent for a foreign government because I met with a Chinese government official. But it's not true!"

"What do you want me to do? I'm not familiar with BC politics or elections and I don't have any contacts in law enforcement here."

"I realize that. But maybe, since you're unknown, you can investigate this without setting off alarm bells with those who did it. I'd like you to find out who's behind it, and whether we can turn the tables on them. I realize it's a long shot, but I'd like you to try."

"You've notified the police, I assume. What are they doing about it?"

"They're investigating me! I was denounced by the staff of another political party, who claim they got an anonymous tip. The force is taking it seriously and ignoring my denials. If I can't give them some evidence I'm being set up, I'll have to resign as MLA and someone else will be elected in my place. The next general election in BC is coming up soon."

"I could investigate for you, but it's going to take some time for me to get up to speed, and Izzie and I were only planning to stay for a week."

"Please give it a try. In law school I remember that you were the one who usually had an unusual way of looking at a problem, and often it paid off in finding a solution."

After the phone call ended, Hamish turned to Izzie. "Looks like our vacation is not going to be solely a vacation for me either! I tried to convince Francis Lee that I wouldn't be of much help, but he was determined to get me on board. So now I'm going to have to learn details about the BC Election Act and how it is applied and policed here. Do you by any chance have any useful contacts here in BC?"

"My law firm's Vancouver office was involved with IPOs–Initial Public Offerings–and securities filings for what was then the Vancouver Stock Exchange, which became the Canadian Venture Exchange, and is now the TSX Venture Exchange and is headquartered in Calgary. Since I've moved to academe I've lost touch, but I could find out if there's someone I know who still works at the Vancouver office. Would that help?"

"Sure. Just about anyone in the province is more knowledgeable than I am about BC electoral issues!"

"Now that I think of it, there was someone on the program of my conference who works at my old firm, Erskine and Associates. I could give him a ring, explain the situation, and see if you could talk to him."

"Great, please do, Izzie. I can arrange to take the Swartz Bay Ferry and meet him at his office."

*****

The receptionist showed Hamish into the office of Izzie's friend, John Carr. The room was without windows, the walls covered with legal volumes, including the back of the entrance door. Hamish felt claustrophobic, since there was no visible exit. It was the proverbial closed room, much appreciated by mystery fans.

"The man stuck out his hand. I'm John Carr, but I go by my initials, JD. So you're Hamish, Izzie's new toy boy, are you?" he said to Hamish with a smile. He was a handsome man with thick curly hair.

Hamish looked at him suspiciously. "Excuse me?"

"Never mind, that was a joke," JD said. "She was an old flame of mine years ago. She used to visit the Vancouver office once a year, reviewing the activities of our securities department and coordinating with Toronto and Montreal. Enough of that, though. What can I help you with?"

"Two days ago I ran into an old friend, Francis Lee, who's a BC MLA. He's now accused by a rival party of taking illegal campaign donations and also being a tool of the Chinese government. He's asked me to look into who might be behind this. He thinks he's been deliberately set up because of his uncompromising views on climate change."

"Can you tell me more about the charges?"

"He received a donation from a company that has operations in BC and Alberta, Wildcat Oil Services, also known as WOS. He thought that the donation was legal–it was under the legal limit of about $1,400 dollars, and came from BC–but the company is in fact headquartered in Calgary. Out-of-province campaign donations apparently are illegal in BC. As for the other issue, he met with some ethnic Chinese voters in his riding, but it turns out that among them was the Chinese consul. Hence the charge, which he denies, of being an agent of a foreign government bent on influencing our elections."

"I see. This does look like dirty tricks. It's suspicious that WOS, which is involved in the oil sands, would make a donation to an advocate for decarbonization. Tell you what, we did the legal filings for their IPO a dozen years ago and I know someone who used to work at the company. He has since joined a law firm in Calgary. I'll give him a ring."

"Please don't tip our hand. If WOS learns that they're being investigated, they'll clam up."

*****

A few hours later, Carr phoned Hamish, who was on the Tsawwassen Ferry on his way back to Victoria. "Here's the story I got from my contact who used to work at WOS. He says that the company is part of an undercover campaign to talk up the benefits of oil and gas extraction and discredit the critics, sometimes using dirty tricks. That's why he quit the firm."

"How extensive is this campaign? Who else is involved?"

"WOS has received millions and millions of dollars from the oil industry to argue their case, and to counteract the negative publicity from the environmental damage. The profits from exploiting Canada's fossil fuels are so enormous that some in the industry will resort to any measure they think will be effective in counteracting opposition. That includes, for instance, understating the negative effects and branding critics eco-terrorists. It's also quite conceivable that WOS could have used a donation to Francis Lee's campaign, which they knew was illegal, to discredit him. It's not clear if they did this on their own or if others are involved."

"How can we find out more about this? I realize I'm asking a lot of you, and probably Francis Lee won't be in a position to pay both of us."

"Don't worry about it. Consider this *pro bono*, my contribution to making the electoral system compliant with the law. So we can work together on this. I think the first thing to do is to find out more about WOS. I can dig out the filings we did, and get a paralegal to research the company–the principals, where they get their profits, and their major shareholders. Then we can go from there. Does that seem like a good plan?"

"Perfect. I'll talk to Francis Lee again to reassure him that we're working on his case. With luck we'll get to the bottom of this and get something to exonerate him of electoral fraud."

*****

"Izzie, you never told me that you had a romantic interest here in BC!"

"Why should I? That was over long ago."

"We were seeing each other at the time–it wasn't that far in the past!"

"Sure, but it's not as if we were married. We decided not to live together because of the possible conflict of interest when you became a judge, if I represented someone who came before your court."

"OK, you're right. It's just that I was taken aback when Carr brought it up. Anyway, it's big of him to help out with this case."

*****

"Here was what my paralegal found out about WOS. Its CEO is someone called Ruben Gallant. I met him when they did the IPO. Quite the booster of the oil sands. From what I remember, he dabbles in politics, but supports whoever is on his side–that is, who is in favour of 'drill, baby, drill'. So he's a big fan of the current Alberta government and an enemy of the Greens, wherever they reside."

"What sort of services does the company provide to the oil industry?"

"They're a sort of jack of all trades, providing technical service in exploration, doing environmental assessments, supplying security guards, and lobbying."

"Do they make a lot of money doing that?"

"They're profitable, but not that much. They don't pay a dividend. Yet the share price has done well, giving a five year average return of 15 percent per annum. Among the largest shareholders are Gallant himself, the big oil companies that developed the oil sands, and Atlantic Venture Capital."

"Is that right? Atlantic Venture Capital is based in Halifax, and it turns out that someone I know used to be an executive there. He's even a client of ours. What a coincidence!" Hamish scratched his head. *How did Jeremy Boswell get involved with the oil sands? Maybe there's something he's not told us about his search for his cousin Tom.*

17

Bar Harbor, Maine

Sean was speaking on the phone with Joe Washington. "We're coming up blank around here now. I wonder if the thieves have decided not to try to sell the outboards in the province because of the arrest you made at Andy's Marina, and have moved their operations to the States. There's a rumour that some of the engines are ending up there. You might alert the US authorities. They could do a more thorough inspection of boats coming into the country from Canada, and might be able to catch the thieves."

"I'll run that by my superiors to see if they think that they can get the cooperation of the Yanks. But you've got to realize that their Department of Homeland Security is mainly concerned with terrorist threats, drug smuggling, and illegal immigration. Thefts of pleasure boats are not high on their agenda. Why don't you go to Maine and pose as someone who's looking for a used engine and isn't too picky about its provenance, as long as the price is right?"

"We'll need a contact involved with policing in the States to arrest the culprits if we find them."

"OK, we can work on that, though getting the cooperation of US law enforcement may be a challenge. I'll give you a list of engines that were stolen here in Nova Scotia, with their serial numbers. If you get a lead, we'll try to apprehend the thieves in Canada, and at the same time send an arrest warrant to the US authorities so they can nab their accomplices there."

"Joe, I have an idea. I have a phone that I picked up in Maine which I use in the US when I travel there. I could advertise online for a used engine in, say, the Bar Harbor area, and give my phone number so that I seem like a legit local buyer. We'll see if the bait attracts any nibbles. The gang can probably locate an engine that matches what I'm looking for, and arrange to have it stolen. I'll play the part of a sucker who doesn't know much about boats and just wants a cheap engine for fishing or water skiing. The insurance company that hired me is willing to go along with my idea, since the thieves seem to operate on both sides of the border."

"That might work. Just keep me informed on a regular basis, Sean."

*****

Sean took the ferry from Yarmouth to Bar Harbor and drove to the rendezvous location. It was a public ramp used to launch small power boats. The man who called him in response to his ad on Craigslist said he would be there around 5 pm. The outboard engine would be on a Carolina skiff tied up next to the launch ramp.

Sean came early, hoping to arrive before the seller, but as he parked his car near the ramp he spotted the boat. A man with a furtive expression was sitting on the gunwale, waiting for him. "You the guy on Craigslist? I'm Bill. Let me show you the Yamaha outboard. He hit the starter, and the engine came to life with a smooth purr. "Runs great. Hop in, we can go for a spin."

They backed away from the dock and headed out toward the bay at a moderate pace. After a minute the man opened up the throttle, and they were speeding along at thirty knots, with the engine showing no sign of strain.

"Sounds good. Mind if I take the tiller?" Sean zig-zagged the boat, accelerating and slowing, to see if the engine showed any sign of stalling. "Yeah, seems fine." He tried to read the serial number from an ID plate, but there did not seem to be one. "OK, we can head back. I'll take her, if you can provide me with a valid title."

As they neared the launch ramp they saw that two agents on an inflatable with the designation "Maine Marine Patrol" were waiting for them. Bill hesitated, but obviously decided that flight was futile, and he tied up at the dock. The agents came over, and one of them addressed Bill and Sean. "You're under arrest. That boat and its engine were taken from the dock of a local boater. You're both accused of dealing in stolen goods."

"But I had nothing to do with that," Sean protested. "This guy answered my advert about a used outboard engine. I had offered to buy a Mercury of this horsepower."

"You are suspected of being an accomplice in the theft. You have the right to remain silent, and to contact a lawyer to represent you."

18

Fort McMurray and Fort McKay

"Francis, I found out something about Wildcat Oil Services, the company in Calgary that made that donation to your campaign. They're heavily involved in greenwashing the oil sands. I suspect that they deliberately tried to discredit you by violating BC's election law. But I don't have any proof. Do you want me to go to Alberta to dig into this some more?"

"Sure, Hamish, if you think there's a chance you'll find something useful."

"All right, I won't bill you for the trip unless I get some results. I spoke to a lawyer whom Izzie knows who was involved in getting the initial financing for the company. He's gotten me an appointment with their CEO in Calgary and also the contact information for a former employee who quit because he didn't like the direction the company was taking. We'll see how it goes."

"In any case, I'll make the case to the electoral commission that their donation doesn't make any sense except as an attempt to incriminate me, given my position on fossil fuels. It could only be a dirty trick. If I return the donation, the electoral commission should drop the charge against me. I'll give you a cheque for the amount, and you could give it to the CEO of WOS. Just make sure you get a receipt."

"I'll do that. Izzie and I will get in some tourism in any case. We want to revisit Banff and Lake Louise, and there's someone we know in Fort McMurray. I've never been there and I'm curious to see for myself what it's like."

*****

"Beth, it's nice of you to meet us at the airport. I'm glad you're still here in Fort McMurray." Hamish and Izzie had flown in from Vancouver. "You've visited WOS. What do you think our best strategy would be to get more info about the company? I'd like to know whether they're planning other dirty tricks. I'm also curious about Jeremy Boswell's relationship with the company. Did he have any contact with them while he was here?"

"I know someone who works at WOS. We can invite her for a meal, and she can tell you what she knows. You could also talk to Tom and Claire Boswell. Let's start there."

Hamish nodded his approval. "You're turning into a real detective, kid. You're a regular V. I. Warshawski."

"Who's that?"

"A bad-ass Chicago detective created by Sara Paretsky."

*****

Flora suggested a restaurant, The Fish Place, which was not far from where she lived, so Beth, Hamish, Lizzie, Tom and Claire joined her at an unpretentious eatery in a strip mall northwest of downtown. "I hope you'll like the seafood, though it may not be up to Nova Scotia standards. We're pretty far from the ocean!"

Hamish shrugged his shoulders. "I'm sure it'll be fine. It's good of you to meet with us, Flora."

"*De nada.* It's my pleasure. Happy to meet with people who know Beth. She's *mi amiga.*"

"So how did you happen to get a job at WOS?"

"Alberta was looking to attract foreign workers, and the job pays a lot more than anything I could get in Mexico. After a couple of years I applied to become a permanent resident, and in a few months I should be a Canadian citizen. I'm a gringo now!"

"I gather from Beth that you have some concerns about what's happening in Fort McMurray. Do you mind telling us about it?"

"I was OK with the place at the beginning, but then came the fire that destroyed much of the city. Again this summer we had an evacuation notice, and now I'm getting more and more nervous about the air quality. I don't really breathe easy here, I'm often gasping for breath. I hope I don't end up like Tom, with lung problems."

"I gather that WOS is involved in selling the oil sands to the public. Do you know anything about that?"

"Nah, the PR work's done by the Head Office in Calgary. But we do the environmental impact assessments, or EIAs, for some of the companies operating here. That's not my department, but I hear some of the technical people talking about it."

Claire interjected. "Requiring extensive assessments is a big factor in convincing the general public that 'companies are environmentally responsible when developing oil and gas resources,' in the words of the Alberta Energy Regulator. It has to approve energy projects in the province. The EIA studies are very detailed, going into the projected impacts on dozens of different emissions and other environmental effects. I'm sure your average citizen never reads any of them, though, as the reports for each project total several thousand pages. If they did, they'd be scared shitless. And yet the AER has approved these projects."

Izzie added, "I understand that an independent study has used a different methodology to assess the overall effect of all of the emissions together, and concluded that air quality is much worse than the EIAs say."

Claire shook her head. "The reasons for the discrepancy are unclear, but further research is underway. The AER may be forced to revise the way assessments are done and their criteria for approval. But the approval decision depends on politics, and the Alberta government shows no sign of wanting to slow down the development of the oil sands. Instead, they attack the renewables industry! That's why the NGO I work for is continuing to alert public opinion and to apply pressure on the government. Only if the province seems to be turning against them will they pay attention."

"What are you planning next to keep the issue in front of them, Claire?"

"We're going to Fort McKay tomorrow to film a documentary on the environment where my mother's people, the Dene, live. It will highlight the degradation of the environment by the oil sands operations there. We hope to get the TV networks to air it, or at least use excerpts in their news clips."

Beth said, "I'd be interested in coming too, if I could."

"Sure, why not? We have a bus for the film crew and their gear, and there's extra space on the bus."

*****

The film crew had come from Edmonton the day before and stayed at one of the downtown Fort McMurray hotels. By 8 am the small yellow school bus was loaded up with their equipment and heading north on highway 63. Claire and Beth sat in the seat behind the driver. It was cloudy now, but the forecast was for a mostly sunny day. The film crew sat in the back, three guys and a gal. They were all about Claire's age, in their mid-to-late twenties. One of the guys was using his camcorder to film the terrain from the bus as they drove by. The others were dozing. Apparently they had partied the night before.

"It should be perfect for filming," Claire said. "The crew is mostly people I met when I studied multimedia journalism at university." The cameras, tripods, booms, and screens were all piled up on the seats at the back.

As they drove north along the Athabasca River, the bleak landscape afforded occasional glimpses of tailings ponds and denuded earth, though most of the oil sands were hidden behind groves of spruce trees. They passed Syncrude's Mildred Lake operation and Suncor's Fort Hills site. Highway 63 became narrower, its name changing to the True North Road before they got to the Fort McKay Indian reserve 174d.

"Stop here," Claire told the driver. "I need to pay my respects to the Dene First Nation chief. I contacted him before and got his permission to do some filming and interviewing people, but I need to check in with him to make sure it's still OK."

The bus pulled up to the First Nation office, and Claire hopped out. Beth turned to talk to the camera crew, who were all awake now. The one who had been filming during the drive introduced himself. "I'm Ted. Claire said she lined up some interviews. We wanted to film the oil sands mining operations also, but they wouldn't let us onto the site. However, we have a secret weapon." He smiled as he pointed to a drone on the seat beside him.

"We're going to see one of the elders. He's waiting for us." Claire consulted a paper that gave directions to his dwelling.

The house was a simple cabin made of logs that consisted of four rooms. Claire knocked and a middle-aged man answered the door immediately and came out onto his porch. "You're Eileen's daughter, aren't you? That poor woman, she passed away so young."

"Yes, I'm Claire. Can we interview you out here? And do you mind if we film it?"

The crew set up their equipment and Claire proceeded to ask Joe for a brief history of the Fort McKay First Nation and their experience with the oil sands.

"Our contact with the white man dates back to the fur trade days. In 1820 the Hudson Bay Company built a trading post at Fort McKay. We coexisted peacefully with them, and in 1899 we signed Treaty 8 with the British Crown, which guarantees us, and I quote, 'the right to continue with our way of life for as long as the sun shines, the grass grows and the rivers flow.' The development of the oil sands started in the 1960s. We were assured that our treaty rights would be respected, so we allowed the oil companies to mine the bitumen. It soon became clear that we would have to fight to protect those rights, and we did. Eventually we decided to embrace the development. The Fort McKay First Nations have established a group of companies that collaborate with outside interests. There's an industrial park here that we helped build. The oil sands have made us wealthy. But we've paid the price in another way. Much of the forests have been dug up, and the air and water quality is no longer what it was. Some of our members have suffered from health issues and have died young."

"So you have seen a lot of changes during your lifetime here, some good, some bad. In your opinion, is the net result a plus or a minus?"

"It depends on your perspective. Many people in Fort McKay see it as a good thing, and other First Nations point to us as an example of sustainable development for them to follow. I don't believe it's a good thing. If I could turn back the clock to before 1960, I would. Then, we lived in partnership with the land. Now, we are accomplices in the rape of Mother Nature. The oil sands mining has trampled our traditions, and endangered our health. But of course you can't stop what people call 'progress.' We signed a new memorandum of understanding with Suncor in March to allow them to extract bitumen on tribal lands."

"Thank you for talking to us, Joe. We're going to drive around the reserve and look at the oil sands before heading back to Fort McMurray."

"There's a girl missing from the reserve. Be careful."

"What happened?"

"We don't know. She's 18 years old. Her mother says she hasn't come back home."

*****

They filmed along the road that led past the hockey arena and First Nation's office. Getting back onto route 63, they crossed the Athabasca and headed north, passing the Fort McKay Industrial Park, a symbol of the First Nation's prosperity. Claire indicated to the driver to turn right onto the road that led to the Muskeg River Mine.

They stopped before reaching the gate that gave access to the mining operation, and Ted launched his drone. After a few minutes he could see on his control screen the scarred ground and the tailings ponds where the boreal forests had once stood. "This will make great footage!" he said. Claire and Beth looked over his shoulder, admiring the clear pictures produced by the drone's camera. He made the drone circle so that they could get a 360 degree view of the site. "That should do it. I'll bring the drone back."

As they were loading it back into the bus, a yellow van with "Wildcat Oil Services" inscribed on it sped up to them. Two men wearing company uniforms got out. One of them, who was older and seemed to be their leader, said, "You don't have permission to film on our site. This is private property. I'll have to ask you for the SD card from your drone's camera." He stuck out his hand.

Claire protested. "You can't do this! I have the permission of the First Nation's chief to film on the reserve! What are you afraid of, exactly? Why can't we film the oil sands?"

The second official, a burly man in his thirties, advanced on Ted, who was still holding the drone. "Give it to me," he said threateningly.

One of the film crew was operating his camcorder, recording the exchange between Claire and the two WOS employees. When one of them noticed this, he backtracked, and spoke in a less threatening tone. "Very well. If you don't give us the footage, we will get a court order forcing you to turn it over and to prevent you from using the video for any public purpose. In addition, we'll get the police to charge you with trespassing." He took a picture of them and their vehicle for identification.

Beth said to Claire, "He's bluffing. Let's get out of here." They and the film crew piled into the bus. The driver slammed the bus into gear and left the security guards standing by their van in a cloud of dust.

Back at Fort McMurray, Claire reported on their day to Tom, Izzie, and Hamish. "WOS really doesn't want any reporting of what goes on at the Muskeg River oil sands site! We thought we would get robbed at gunpoint, but fortunately we managed to get away. Our drone footage will make a great video!"

19

Calgary

Hamish turned to Izzie as they were disembarking at Calgary airport after their short flight from Fort McMurray. "Your friend JD Carr has set up a meeting with the president and CEO of Wildcat Oil Services, Ruben Gallant. Apparently Carr has known him since he helped launch the company. It would be helpful if you came along, if you don't mind."

"As long as you don't expect me to take notes!" She laughed.

They took a cab to The Bow, and after checking in with the reception desk at ground level, they were met by Gallant's assistant and taken up to his office. The view of downtown Calgary and the Rockies in the distance was spectacular. Gallant rose from his chair and came around his desk to welcome them. After shaking hands, he invited them to sit on a couch, while he took an armchair next to it.

"JD didn't mention the reason for your visit. But he's been involved with the company from day one, and a friend of his is a friend of mine! So how can I help?"

Hamish smiled. "We're taking advantage of a holiday in BC and Alberta to learn more about Canada's Western Provinces–in particular the booming energy sector. How do you see things developing, given concerns about climate change and the environmental degradation associated with exploiting the oil sands? At the same time, oil companies have ramped up production, making Canada the fourth largest oil exporter in the world. Are these two trends going to collide at some point, and, if so, what will it mean for Alberta?"

"Wow, you ask tough questions! You probably know what WOS does, but let me give you a short summary. The oil services we provide include doing environmental impact assessments that need to be prepared and submitted to the Alberta Energy Regulator before new projects are approved, and doing PR work. I can unequivocally say that our oil sector is as respectful of the environment as any in the world. It is true that we contribute substantially to carbon emissions, but we are on the verge of implementing a major technological advance, namely carbon capture and storage. If put in place as planned, it should make our emissions targets achievable by 2050."

"But if I understand correctly, the technology is largely unproven, and it's unclear whether it can be scaled up enough to offset almost completely the emissions from the oil sands, as industry sources contend. The *in situ* extraction burns one hell of a lot of natural gas to create the steam needed to melt the bitumen."

"I'm confident that any technical problems that may arise can be solved. The critics are never satisfied. We give them solutions and they make up other objections! The world needs energy, and we as a country are well positioned to provide it. That won't change. The government of Alberta is right just to ignore the naysayers."

Hamish let his scepticism show on his face. "I have another purpose for my visit. A friend of mine, Francis Lee, has asked me to return a donation that you made to his re-election campaign in the BC election. He thinks it must be a mistake, since he is dead-set against exploiting the oil sands on environmental grounds."

Gallant looked puzzled. "Francis Lee? The name doesn't ring a bell. I don't recall making such a donation myself."

"Perhaps I should have said that it came from your company, not you directly. I gather WOS is involved in attacking the critics of the oil sands. Your company's contribution to my friend's campaign violated BC electoral law because it came from out of province. It seems obvious that it was made in order to discredit him. The MLA is now at risk of losing his seat as a result."

Gallant face sported the beginnings of a smirk, which he did his best to hide. "Oh my, that's too bad. Of course we try to help out politicians who support sustainable development of Canada's energy resources, but perhaps my staff didn't do sufficient research in this case."

"I would like you to give me a receipt for this cheque from Francis Lee, saying that the donation to his campaign was made in error."

Gallant hesitated, then acceded to Hamish's request. "I'll get my staff to do that." He gave instructions over the intercom to his assistant.

Hamish continued. "Some of your employees recently threatened activists who were filming at an oil sands mine in Fort McKay. Is this also part of your PR work for the oil sands?"

Gallant's initially friendly manner had morphed into an annoyed pout. "How dare you come here and accuse me in this way! We're legitimately defending the public's safety as well as the interests of companies operating in the oil sands. The industry has to protect itself against eco-terrorists, and we have to keep the public away from our earth moving equipment so as to prevent accidents!" He rose from his chair. "That's it, our meeting is finished." He strode to his desk and pressed the call button for his assistant. "Show these two out," he told her.

*****

"I don't think we learned anything new, did we?" Izzie asked Hamish, after they were escorted off the elevator at ground level. "Though his reaction confirmed that his company is involved in dirty tricks against the activists. Unfortunately, there's not much we can do about it."

"At least Francis Lee got the return of his donation accepted by Gallant with a note saying that it had been made in error. The elections board should as a result take his word that he took the WOS contribution unwittingly. Any research into the company would discover that their position is 180 degrees off that of Francis and other climate activists. As for the China interference accusation, I wonder if there's a link to WOS as well. China is heavily invested in the oil sands through its state-owned company, CNOOC, as well as in shale gas in BC. They may have coordinated with WOS in planting their consul among those meeting with Francis in order to discredit him."

"That's possible, but I don't see how we could prove it. Gallant will certainly refuse to talk to us again. At least foreign interference in our elections is now taken seriously. I expect that the RCMP will investigate the incident with Francis Lee, and hopefully they'll exonerate him."

"Let's talk to the lawyer here in town that JD Carr mentioned, who used to work for WOS. Maybe he can give us some useful info, even though he hasn't worked for them for some time."

20

Archibald Squire greeted Hamish and Izzie at the entrance to his office, located in a busy mall just outside downtown. "My receptionist is sick today, so I'm all alone here," he said with an apologetic smile. The sign outside said that he specialized in personal and job-related health and injury cases.

"It's nice of you to see us on such short notice," Hamish said. "We just spent half an hour talking with Ruben Gallant. He threw us out of his office after denying any wrongdoing by WOS when I suggested that his firm was resorting to dirty tricks against opponents of the oil sands. JD Carr says you know otherwise."

"I spent five years there, in the early days just after it was founded. At first, the company focused on providing logistics services–expertise in drilling, mining, and processing the oil sands. As a lawyer, there wasn't much I had to do except deal with liability issues, such as health claims. Then Ruben met with some Chinese investors who were keen to buy into the company. As the founder, Ruben still owned a lot of stock and he was keen to get rid of some of it without hurting the share price. The Chinese viewed the oil sands as a great opportunity. They also had a hidden agenda, which was to use the company as a vehicle for PRC government policy. In particular, they wanted to boost the electoral chances of candidates–both federal and provincial–who supported mining the oil sands and other Chinese government policies, and to undermine their critics."

"So WOS became a vehicle for foreign interference in Canadian elections?"

"That's right. That was the quid pro quo for their buying Ruben's shares. After that, WOS became much more involved in advocacy than in providing logistics, though it continued with the latter. We donated money to the campaigns of boosters of the oil sands, including those who welcomed foreign investment–especially from China. At this point, I decided to leave the company."

"Did you complain to Elections Canada or the provincial agencies?"

"I talked to the relevant people, but there was little interest in what I had to say at that time. It's only recently that Canadian governments have taken the threats to democracy from foreign interference seriously."

Izzie interrupted. "It sounds as though Ruben Gallant violated securities laws when he brought in the Chinese investors, though the Alberta Securities Commission might not be too eager to charge them."

Hamish turned to Squire: "Can anything be done about it now?"

"I doubt if allegations about events more than a decade ago will get any traction today. The current Alberta government in any case has no quarrel with the positions taken by WOS with respect to the oil sands. But BC is another story. It sounds as though your friend was deliberately targeted by WOS, in coordination with the Chinese consul there. If you can prove that a Chinese company or group of Chinese investors is a large shareholder in WOS, then alerting the BC electoral commission should cause them to suspect foul play. That should get your friend off the hook. I'll provide them with the information that I have if they contact me."

"Thank you very much. We'll be in touch."

*****

It was a nice day, and Hamish and Izzie walked back to their hotel, admiring the tall buildings and the free LRT public transit in downtown Calgary. "It's certainly changed a lot over the past few decades," Izzie said. "I remember when it deserved its name of Cow Town. Not any more."

Hamish was visibly more relaxed than he had been after their visit with the CEO of WOS. "That was very helpful. In any case, we've done what we could for Francis. Now let's have some fun here before we go back east."

"I agree. What do you have in mind?"

"Let's rent a car and drive to Banff and Lake Louise. We can do some hiking there. The leaves on the trees are starting to turn red and yellow, and the tourists have thinned out. Too bad that Jasper's still rebuilding after the forest fires. After a few days, we'll fly back to Halifax."

21

Fort McMurray and Fort McKay

"Beth and I will edit the drone footage and see if we can interest the networks in a documentary about the oil sands," Claire told Sarah, the director of AOSCP. "At least we didn't have our video confiscated. It looked like the guards would force us to turn the memory card over to them, but the fact that we were filming the encounter with the WOS employees got them to back off."

They scrolled through the video, making a copy that eliminated the uninteresting parts and was spliced to the interview with the Dene elder, the footage taken from the bus on their drive north, and their discussion with the security guards. Claire said, "I think this should be of interest to shows like *The Nature of Things* on the CBC. True, there's nothing new here, but the issues it raises are still topical—more and more so, given the ramp up in oil sands production and increased frequency of climate disasters."

111

Beth was looking intently at the screen. "Wait a sec. Would you back up a bit? There's something that caught my eye in the drone footage. There–that looks like a human body floating in the tailings pond!"

"Are you sure? Maybe it's nothing. It certainly looks like a body, but it could be a log. We need to look at it more carefully." She zoomed in on the point where Beth had pointed. "No, the resolution isn't enough to identify it. "

"OK, let's take Ted and his drone up there again to have another look before we do anything about it."

*****

Claire was driving her father's old RAV4. "We'd better not park near the gate this time. There's a place we can pull into that's not visible from the road. We can launch the drone from there."

Ted manipulated the controls so that the drone flew high above the mine until it got to the tailings pond. Then he descended enough so that they could examine the pond's surface. The oily water was covered in scum. "It's hard to pick out objects on the pond. After they separate the oil from the sand using steam, the water runoff is really dirty. I'll make the drone circle around. But the tailings pond is about 1 km by 2 km, so there's a lot to survey."

After half an hour they had not spotted anything resembling a body in the pond. "Uh-oh, here comes a security guard. I see him from the drone approaching the tailings pond using the road. Wait! He has a shotgun!" They heard a distant blast and the drone feed went dead.

"OK, that's enough," Claire yelled. "Let's get out of here!"

They pulled back onto the road that led to route 63. But as they approached the intersection, they saw that a security van had parked across the road. Standing in front of it was a man with a shotgun. Claire made a quick u-turn, going back the way they came, the car heeling over as she accelerated away. "I know there's a hotel along this road. Hopefully we'll be safe there. Aside from that, we're hemmed in. At the end of this road is the gate to the mine, and they'll catch us there!"

Claire glanced in the rear-view mirror, spotting the security van following them. "They're after us now!" In another half kilometre a sign indicated the entrance on the right, and they sped down the driveway, Claire parking among the vehicles behind the lodge building. She took out her cell phone and called the First Nation's office. "This is Claire. Can you come to The Lodge ASAP? We're being hassled again by security for taking photos of the mine. They shot our drone out of the sky!"

"We'll send a Peace Officer. Just hold on, don't do anything to provoke the security guards."

A few seconds later the security van emerged from around the building, cruising slowly. Claire, Beth, and Ted huddled low in their seats, in the hope of not being spotted. Their little car was parked between two large pickup trucks, and was not visible from the side. The van passed behind them, then stopped and backed up, blocking the rear of Claire's car. Looking into her side-view mirror, Claire saw the driver get out and walk towards her car's door. He was not carrying his shotgun but he had a pistol in a holster on his belt. She locked the car's doors, and refused to open the window when he tapped upon it.

"This is going to get ugly," Beth said. But at that moment a cruiser with an emblem identifying its occupant as a Fort McKay Peace Officer pulled up. A man in uniform got out of the cruiser. The security guard addressed him with a scowl. "You're off the reserve here. The mine is our responsibility. So butt out!"

"These are our traditional tribal lands. We have the right to continue to use them. And you have no policing powers. So what's the problem here?"

"They were trespassing, flying their drone over the mine site."

"And what's the problem with that?"

"They were interfering with our operations. They didn't have permission."

"OK, if you think some crime was committed, then take it up with the RCMP. Otherwise, leave them alone!" He glared at the security guard, who backed down. He walked back to his van, but before getting in said to the Peace Officer, "You win this time, but don't think that you'll get your way. We have the resources to buy out you and your band any time we want!" He drove away, narrowly missing the cruiser as he sped away, leaving a black stripe of rubber on the pavement.

Claire warmly thanked the Peace Officer, who had introduced himself as Migizi. "We were here filming two days ago, and when we went over the video we saw what looked to be a body in the tailings pond. We came back to investigate. Do you know anything about that?"

"As the guy said, we don't patrol this area. But there's a missing girl. She's only 18. We're trying to find her."

Ted rustled through his gear. "It's a good thing I bought a spare drone. It's an old one. I hope it still works."

Ted launched the drone, which responded as it should, and sent it high above the pond. Migizi looked intently at the screen. "Can we look more closely there?" He pointed to a small bay where some debris had accumulated.

As the drone descended they looked with dread as a bloated human body came into focus. "I'm going to notify the RCMP right away," Migizi said, swallowing the bile that had risen in his throat. "It seems very likely that it's Beverly, the missing girl."

*****

Beth called Sean's cell number, and having received no reply, left him a message. "Sean, it's starting to get messy out here. We've found the body of a missing indigenous girl in a tailings pond next to an oil sands mining site, and we're getting harassed by a firm that provides security. It may be time to call in the cavalry! Any chance you can make it out here? Bye for now."

22

Bar Harbor, Maine

Sean was sitting disconsolate in a police holding cell in Bar Harbor. *I should never have agreed to Joe Washington's suggestion. They won't let me call him. They pretend never to have heard of the RCMP! I'll have to use my one phone call to hire a local lawyer, someone they suggest since I don't know a soul here.*

After a wait of more than an hour, Sean was able to meet face to face with the lawyer whose name he was given. He was a young man, seemingly just out of law school. Sean wondered if he had even passed the bar exam. He wore jeans and a hoodie, and Sean did not find this very reassuring in someone he depended on to get out of jail.

"My name is Devon Charles, and I will represent you. You're accused of being involved in the theft of a boat and outboard motor. Can you tell me about it?"

Sean contained his temper with difficulty. "I was not criminally involved with thieves, I just got an answer to my ad on Craigslist, where I said that I was looking for a particular outboard motor! Someone brought one around for me to look at.

116

I'd never seen him before. I didn't know the boat and motor were stolen."

"Apparently the police are charging you because they suspect that there's a gang whose technique is to invite people to post a seemingly legitimate request online, which is actually a way of telling the gang members to steal that item. Then the sale goes through at a mutually agreed location and price."

"That's why I posted the ad. We had some thefts in Canada, which an insurance company hired me to look into. We heard rumours that the boats and/or motors were being sold in the US. So I posted the ad. When I got a response I came here to investigate."

"But you didn't notify Maine police of this?"

"I was dealing with our police, the RCMP. I'll give you the contact information for the person I was talking to. It was his job to notify the authorities here. Anyway, I did nothing wrong."

"OK, I'll try to get you released. But I don't promise that it will work. The cops here don't take kindly to other forces operating here without notifying them, much less private detectives. They may want to teach you Canadians a lesson. Besides, I expect you entered the US under false pretences. Did you notify the border security agent that you wanted to meet a potential boat thief?"

Sean looked stunned. "No, I just said I wanted to visit Bar Harbor!"

Charles gathered his papers and stood up. "I'll be in touch."

Sean was returned to the holding cell. There were three other men there, walking up and down, stretching, and looking bored. Sean thought that they must not be first offenders, since they didn't look panicked or particularly unhappy. *They seem right at home here.*

One of them came over to Sean and spoke to him in a strong Maine accent. "What you in for? You're not from around here, are you?"

"No, I'm from Canada."

"Canada, eh?" He burst out laughing. "What the fuck are you doing here?"

"I was going to buy an outboard motor, and the Maine Marine Patrol arrested me and the seller. I didn't commit any crime."

"You sure you weren't going to fence the stolen goods? No, never mind, don't answer that. But that's what the cops will be thinking. Especially since you come from Canada. There's a lot of stuff that crosses the border and nobody hears anything about after that."

"Is that right? I thought the border was pretty tight."

"No, it's a great way of laundering money or getting rid of stolen goods. Get it out of the sight of the cops who are looking for you. If you're in another jurisdiction, especially across the border, your chances of getting away with it go way up!"

"You think that's what the boat thieves do? They hope to sucker residents of another state or country, and avoid the local police?"

"Hey, you didn't hear it from me, but it's a no-brainer. It's big business now. The border officers are just concerned with wetbacks and drugs, and not much else. Just look at all those stolen cars that get shipped out in containers and end up someplace foreign, whether it's Abu Dhabi or Alberta!"

"So who runs this? Or is it a lot of freelancers who just get lucky in finding a sucker who's not particular about where the stuff they buy came from?"

"Some of both. There's an App, outboards.com, that thieves can use to locate the engines for potential buyers. Again, you didn't hear it from me." The man turned his back and walked back to his chums, who had been listening to their conversation. He made a gesture to reassure them that Sean wasn't likely to snitch on them.

*****

Sean spent another hour doing nothing except fretting. A guard came to the cell and called his name. "Come with me to the interview room. The Marine Patrol officer in charge of the case wants to question you."

"Will my lawyer be there?"

"I wouldn't know. Not my business."

As it happened, Devon Charles was waiting for him in the interview room, a ten foot square space with a table and four chairs. "You may be in luck. They want to make sure you're giving them all the information you have. If it checks out, then I think they'll let you go. I phoned Joe Washington at your RCMP, and he spoke to the Maine police. They should be on board."

The Marine Patrol Officer came into the room, a heavy set, tired looking man. He motioned them to sit. "Now, Mr. Carroll, what exactly did you think you were doing pursuing criminals here in Maine without authorization?"

Sean turned to Devon, who raised his eyebrows but didn't say anything.

"I was hoping to find out something about a ring of boat thieves that we think are operating in both Canada and the US. The RCMP doesn't have the resources to investigate. I was hired by a marina owner and an insurance company, and I helped to nab one set of thieves near to where I live. So the RCMP suggested I pose as a boater wanting to buy a certain sized engine. I got a response to my advert from someone in the States and I came to meet with the seller."

"Were you going to purchase the stolen engine?"

"No, I was going to alert the authorities that I thought the engine was stolen. That's as far as it went. I never got a chance, since you apprehended me as well as the seller."

"If you'd talked to us first, we would have told you to lay off. We're investigating a slew of boat thefts ourselves. We've been trying to identify members of the gang without alerting them first. You got in the way of our investigation. Actually, now that we're aware that the gang extends to Canada, perhaps we can make better progress. We'll tighten up our patrols and with the help of your coast guard search more of the boats crossing the border. Tell me something else: what do you know about outboards.com?"

"Nothing, but one of the thieves we caught in Canada had a listing of different outboard engines that apparently was downloaded from their site."

"Well, the guy who showed you the boat in Bar Harbor had a card in his wallet with their web address on it, as well as a password."

He got up and walked towards the door. He nodded in Sean's direction. "You're free to go."

*****

After taking a cab to the boat launch site to retrieve his car, he took the ferry back to Yarmouth. Before going home to Ashcroft he stopped at the RCMP's Lunenburg Detachment Office. Joe Washington came down right away to meet him as soon as he was informed of his presence by the receptionist.

Sean didn't give him time to speak. "Thanks to you, Joe, I've learned what it's like to be held in a US prison! If only you'd notified the Maine Marine Patrol of what we were doing, none of this would have happened!"

"Yes, I'm sorry, Sean. But the good news is that now we have the cooperation of the Maine police. I've filled in the insurance company about what's happened, and they're pleased that things are moving forward. I'm sure they'll compensate you for your time in the States. And Andy is no longer being threatened with having his insurance pulled."

"As of now, I'm not having anything more to do with this case." Without another word, Sean turned and headed out the door.

When he got back to The Oaks, he listened to Beth's message. *Damn, I hope it's not too late to give her a hand out in Alberta.* He left a message for her to call him.

23

Fort McMurray and Fort McKay

"The missing girl was in fact Beverly." Claire was talking to Beth at the AOSCP trailer. "The RCMP has confirmed that the body we spotted in the tailings pond was hers. They don't know or won't say how she got there."

"This puts the actions of the WOS security guards in a new light. In particular, why in the hell did they shoot down our drone? Did they know that the body was there? And if it wasn't an accident, who killed her?"

"Well, you're the detective, Beth. Find out!"

"I'm going to talk to Flora. She may have heard something at WOS. Somehow they seem to be in the middle of this."

*****

Beth, Claire, and Flora met at the Fish Place to discuss what to do over a meal. Beth said to her friends, "Let me treat you to dinner. I'm going to claim it as expenses from that so-and-so Jeremy. I think he owes it to us."

Claire laughed. "I guess that's one way of getting some of his money, since he's made it clear that my father and I aren't getting any inheritance!"

Beth turned to Flora. "What we'd really like to know is what's going on at WOS. Was there any scuttlebut at work about the incident up in Fort McKay?"

"The guards live on site, so we don't talk to them much, only when they come down to the office from Fort McKay. But I hear some talk. My boss is worried. Are you going to sue them for destroying your drone?"

Claire answered. "It belongs to the guys I know in the journalism program at the university, and, yes, I think they're talking to WOS about compensation and will sue if they don't get it. But I've also heard some talk from my friends on the reserve. They say that Beverly was hanging out at one of the lodges, was seen drinking there and mixing with the oil sands workers. She could have known the guards too. I think we should go back up there and talk to people there, also maybe with the Peace Officer, Migizi."

"What about the RCMP?"

"The Mounties probably aren't going to be willing to reveal anything to us, and they don't want us looking into this. Flora, keep your ear to the ground, see if you can find out something about the guards."

"OK, I'll let you know if I hear anything."

*****

Claire and Beth were wearing their out-on-the-town clothes and drew a few leers as they walked into the bar at The Lodge in Fort McKay, in whose parking lot the WOS security guard had confronted them a few days before. It was Friday night, and it was filling up with guys who wanted to unwind after work.

They sat at the bar, and ordered a couple of light beers. There were a few other women sitting together at tables, but the clientele was mainly men. "We don't want to overdo it, but we've got to drink something to show we're legitimate customers," Beth said to Claire. She turned to the bartender, who had just served another client. "Tell me, is it busy every night, or just weekends? Mainly people who live here and on the reserve?"

The barman looked down the counter first, to make sure he wasn't neglecting other customers eager to order. "It depends. We mainly get people who live here at The Lodge while they work at the oil sands. But the shifts are staggered, so everyone isn't working the normal workweek and partying on the weekend."

"I hear there was a girl from the reserve who was found in a tailings pond. Did she ever come in here?"

"It's possible. Why are you asking? Are you up here for the weekend, staying at The Lodge?"

"Nah, we're just passing through."

He raised his eyebrows. "Not much tourism here. But if you're looking for guys, you gals have come to the right place." He gave them a wink that suggested that he thought that they might be hookers.

Beth changed gears. "Actually, we're the ones who discovered the body of the indigenous girl, while looking over drone footage. So we have sort of a personal interest in what happened to her. Anything you can tell us would be helpful. Her case won't get much attention from the cops, judging by what's happened to other indigenous women in Western Canada."

He looked at Claire, trying to judge whether she was from one of the First Nations. "I get what you're saying. I might have seen her here once or twice. She was talking to one of the security guards, I think. Then I didn't see her anymore, or the guy either."

"Can you identify any of the guys she was with?"

"I wouldn't know their names, but if I see them come in, I'll let you know." He moved down the bar to serve another client.

Claire spotted someone she knew from the reserve, and waved to him—a heavy-set, middle aged man. He was wearing work clothes: blue overalls and reinforced leather boots. He came over and gave her a hug. "How's Eileen's daughter? Are you making out OK? And how's Tom?"

"My father and I are doing fine, George. So, are you working at the mine now?"

"Yeah, I'm driving one of the big 400 tonne Cats from the mine to the processing plant. I just got off my shift. I usually grab a beer before going home and showering. Need something to unwind."

"This is my friend Beth. We're trying to find out what might have happened to Beverly. We actually were the ones to spot her in a video taken from a drone."

"It's a sad business. I just wish her mother had kept tabs on her. She shouldn't have been allowed to come here."

"So, is the reserve's Peace Officer going to investigate this?"

"Nah, it's the job of the RCMP, if there's a major crime. I can't understand why she would want to be in the area near the tailings pond. There's nothing there but dirt and bitumen. But I guess her body might have been dumped there."

"How would she have gotten into the mine? There's a high fence all around it."

"I dunno, but it seems likely that she came in with one of the workmen, either a driver like myself or a shovel operator. Or one of the supervisors."

"What about a security guard?"

"Possibly, but they usually patrol the outside perimeter."

"Do you know if there is CCTV surveillance footage of the mine?"

"There's bound to be. But it's a big place. I doubt they can cover it all."

As they were talking, the security guard who had accosted them in the parking lot came in the door. He wasn't wearing a uniform, so it seemed unlikely that he had just gotten off his shift. Without looking toward Beth and Claire, he walked to the other end of the bar, and spoke to a man sitting there. The two of them went over to a booth, where they sat and chatted in low voices.

The bartender came over to Beth and said, "That's one of the guys I remember seeing her with. The one who just came in." He nodded towards the booth.

Beth looked at Claire, raising her eyebrows. "How're we going to do this? We need to find out more about the security guards. I don't think he saw me in the car the other day. I'll go over there and sit in the booth behind them. Maybe I can pick up some of their conversation. You stay here with George. Try not to be conspicuous. Hopefully he won't look over in your direction." She nodded to George as she eased off her bar stool and strolled over to where the two men were talking.

The booths were separated by a wood partition that went part of the way to the ceiling, concealing occupants from those in neighbouring booths. Beth quietly slipped into the one next to theirs. Voices were muffled, but she could make out most of what they said.

"I tell ya, they're onto us. We shouldn't have shot down the drone, or we shoulda just grabbed the memory stick so that they wouldn't have any proof."

"Nah, you're getting paranoid. We were just doing our job. They had no right to fly that drone over the mine site, and tough luck if it got shot down. That's what we'll keep saying if someone asks. Hang tough."

"So there's nothing on the body linking me to her? Yer sure?"

"Yeah, don't worry. Let's order something to drink." He waved over a waitress. She took their orders, then went to the next booth and asked Beth what she wanted. One of the men craned his neck, spotting her. "Shit, there was someone listening. Let's get outta here." They got up and hurried toward the back door.

Beth followed them out, waving frantically to Claire and George to follow her. They reached the parking lot just as the two men got into their car, a late model Toyota with no markings on it. Beth pulled out her camera and took a picture of the car's licence plate.

*****

As Beth and Claire drove back to Fort McMurray, they discussed what they should do now. Beth offered: "I think we should go to the RCMP. This whole mess is too much for us to handle. I tried to get some help from another detective at the agency I work for, but we've been playing phone tag and he won't get here any time soon."

Claire looked sceptical. "When we made complaints to the RCMP in the past about being harassed at our oil sands protests, they just shrugged us off. And they hardly bother to investigate the disappearance of indigenous women."

"Those two men are clearly implicated in some way in Beverly's death. I can show them the licence number, they should be able to track them down."

"Good luck with that! But I guess it's worth a try."

The RCMP's Wood Buffalo Detachment, with responsibility for a vast territory including the oil sands and the Chipewyan Prairie First Nation, was located in a sprawling multi level building on Paquette Avenue in Fort McMurray. They parked in front, walked past an array of flags, and entered the building. Beth told the receptionist, "We're here because we have some information about the death of an indigenous woman in Fort McKay. Could we speak to an investigator on the case?"

The woman wearing a phone headset at the desk nodded. She keyed in a few numbers and spoke briefly into the phone. Turning to Beth and Claire, she said, "Please sit. Someone will come to see you shortly."

After about 15 minutes a young man in uniform emerged from the elevator and came over to them. "Are you here about the death of Beverly Racette? I'm Constable Brown. Would you come with me, please." He led them to his office on the second floor, a small windowless rectangular room. He motioned to two chairs in front of his desk, while he sat behind it in his swivel chair. "Now, what can I do for you?"

Claire answered indignantly. "It's the other way around: it's about what we can do for you! We have some information about her death. We were the ones who discovered the body while filming from a drone, and we have identified one of the security guards who attempted to take the drone footage from us."

"So you were illegally filming on private property? You realize that none of that information can be used in a court of law, and the operator of the mine can sue you for invasion of privacy."

Beth cut in. "But surely you can use this information to investigate whether a crime has been committed! And I overheard the two men admitting that they were involved but were going to cover it up."

"Oh, and what crime was that?"

"They didn't say. They were just afraid that you would catch on to what they'd done and find some evidence on the body linking them to her. They clearly feared that you would find out what had happened to the girl. Has a post-mortem been done? What did she die of?"

"I'm not at liberty to say. But we're not actively investigating her death. As for the security guards, it seems clear to me that they were only doing their job, which is to prevent unauthorized access to the oil sands. So I would like to ask you a few questions about the dead woman. Was she planning a sit-in at the site? We understand that she was part of a cell that aimed to disrupt the oil sands mining. Do you know any of her confederates?"

Beth bridled. "What are you trying to do, blame the victim? Anyway, we have no knowledge of the reason why she was there. Surely you need to investigate her death to find out?"

Brown shook his head in annoyance. "If you can't help me further, I'll get back to my work. I'll see you out." He got up, opened the door for them, and escorted them to the elevator.

As they left the building, Claire said to Beth, "That went just as I expected. They're more concerned with the privacy rights of the oil companies than with crimes against indigenous women. According to him, we're the criminals, not the guards."

24

Ashcroft-by-the-Sea

"You wouldn't believe what I've been through! I was arrested by Maine police because Joe Washington didn't notify them that I was trying to track down boat thieves." Sean had called Hamish, who was walking around Banff with Izzie while speaking on his cellphone. "Anyway, I'm done with the boat theft gig. I think Andy is OK now with the insurance companies. I'll just see if I can find the website the thieves seem to use. Then I hope to join Beth in Alberta, since it looks like she's staying there for a while."

"Sounds good. She's a little dynamo, that girl. She's gotten her teeth into the oil sands and won't let go!"

*****

Let's see, the printouts on Bud Reagan's boat were off the out-boards.com website. Let me see if I can find it.

When Sean got on, the site seemed to be what it pretended to be, a source of information about different makes and models of outboard engines, with photos and reviews. The menu at the top of the home page included a Login tab. When Sean clicked on it, an error message came back saying "You are not authorized to enter this site." *Hmm, I wasn't even prompted to enter a userid or password. I wonder if there's another site that's accessible only through the Tor browser.* Tor, which stood for The Onion Router, allowed anonymous access to sites with the suffix .onion, preventing any tracking, surveillance, or censorship. Those sites were informally known as the dark web, because they could not be accessed by the standard internet browsers or easily tracked because they were routed in a different way from the World Wide Web.

Sean was familiar with the dark web from his job as internet specialist for a company based in Chicago. He had downloaded a Tor browser to his laptop, though he did not generally use it. Now he tried to search for outboards.onion but got instead a much more complicated URL that had "outboards.com" as a prefix and ".onion" as a suffix, with a lot of random characters in between.

Hmm, that's interesting: there's the same information as on the public site, but additional tabs, "subscribe to registration directories" and "buy/sell/trade." Let's see what that's about. The first page indicated that by paying a hundred dollars, the user could have one-time access to a listing of those who lived in a particular area who were registered as having purchased a particular type of outboard engine, along with their contact details and the serial number of the engine. *I'll bet someone hacked into the manufacturers' computers to get that information. Now I see how the thefts are coordinated! There's no face-to-face contact. It's through the hefty fee that the hackers monetize their information. They don't have anything to do with the thefts themselves. Instead, the thieves inde-*

pendently access the site in order to steal an engine for their own use or to sell it, for instance in response to a want-ad. Ingenious!

Sean did not pursue this further, except to notify the RCMP what he had found. "Joe, you might want to alert the US authorities as well. They probably have the best chance of closing down that website, and investigating the hacking of owner registration databases."

"Good work, Sean. We'll coordinate with them, and find a way to shut this down."

Sean then tried to contact Beth, but he was unable to get through. *She's either not in range or her phone isn't on. I'll try again later.*

*****

Sean finally managed to communicate with her by phone. "Beth, how long are you planning to stay out there? Jeremy Boswell's no longer paying the detective agency for our services, so you're living on your own dime."

"I'm investigating the death of an indigenous woman up in Fort McKay, with the help of Claire, Tom Boswell's daughter. It's really important for us to engage with the RCMP, since it forces them to get off their asses and do a serious job investigating it. Otherwise, they will just let it become one of many unsolved cases of deaths of indigenous women."

"Beth, you're going way beyond the purpose of your trip to Alberta. Let the police do their job! Aside from that, I'd be happy to come out there to join you. I've been wanting to explore Alberta for some time. This would be a good opportunity."

"Sean, in the end I'd rather you didn't. You're just going to distract me from the investigation. Claire is relying on me to help. I need to focus on that, not on sightseeing. I'll keep you up to date. Just give me another week or so."

"OK, Beth, whatever works for you," Sean said in a disappointed tone. "But keep in mind that doing police work is outside your mandate and Cameron and Carroll, Investigators is not going to back you up."

25

Fort McMurray and Fort McKay

"**B**eth, this is Flora. I kept my ear to the ground, as you told me to do, and guess what I learned. My boss here in Fort McMurray has changed the security guards up at the Muskeg River Mine in Fort McKay. A guy from the RCMP's office came to see him. The guards have cleared out."

"Any idea of where they went?"

"*Nada.* I'm guessing they were told to disappear. The two new guards are already on the job in Fort McKay."

"Thanks, Flora. You've done me a solid!"

*****

"Migizi, that means Eagle in Dene, right?" Claire asked. She had reached him by phone in the Peace Officer's cruiser. "I've a question for you, you who have eagle eyes. What happened after we looked at the drone footage of Beverly's body in the tailings pond? You talked to the RCMP. What did they say when

135

you reported the body? Did they do any investigating afterwards?"

"We recently had an RCMP community outreach person assigned to our office in the Fort McKay First Nation administration building. I went to see him and said we had found a body that might be hers. She'd been reported missing the week before. He said he'd look into it, and they retrieved her body from the tailings pond. That's the last I heard of it, except that they released her body to her mother the next day. There's a burial service tomorrow."

"So, no autopsy? Did they discover how she got into the tailings pond?"

"Not that I know of. But the RCMP doesn't involve us in police investigations. That would be done out of Fort McMurray in any case."

"And you haven't seen anybody from there poking around?"

"An RCMP Constable drove up to examine the site where the body was found, but I didn't see any other evidence of an investigation."

"So, as usual, the death of an indigenous woman doesn't concern them much!"

"It seems that way."

"By the way, I'm going to come up there for the funeral. I want to offer my condolences to Beverly's mother. I remember meeting her when my mother was still alive and we visited family on the reserve."

"OK, see you tomorrow."

*****

Claire and Beth drove north to Fort McKay once again in Claire's father's car. "I hope we'll be on time. They were a little vague about the time of the service and the interment. I want to talk to Beverly's mother, Marie Racette. She must know something about what happened to her daughter. Thanks for coming with me, Beth."

"I wouldn't want you to do this drive alone. It's a long way to travel by yourself. Besides, I want to investigate Beverly's death, since the RCMP obviously doesn't take seriously the possibility that it's a crime."

The service had already started when Claire and Beth slipped into a pew at the back of the church. Claire recognized a few faces, including that of Marie Racette sitting at the front. Just behind her was Migizi, the Peace Officer, and a man wearing an RCMP uniform. *He must be their community engagement officer,* she thought.

After a brief religious service, several older men and women of the reserve spoke of the dead girl, some in English and others in Dene. Though Claire knew a few of the words, she had trouble following since she had not lived long in Fort McKay, and her mother had passed away too early to teach her much of her language. At the end, Beverly's friend Sadie rose and addressed those attending. With tears in her eyes, she spoke of her long friendship with her. "She was my best friend. We were working together to expose the evils of oil sands mining. Now she's dead!" At this point, she choked up and ran back to her pew.

After the ceremony, the coffin was hoisted by half a dozen First Nation men and carried to the Fort McKay cemetery to be interred. Claire and Beth stayed discreetly back. Beth said quietly, "I'd like to talk to Sadie. Do you know her family?"

"No, I don't. And I don't see Sadie. I guess she was too upset to come to the interment."

They waited to approach Beverly's mother once most of the others had left, many of them after exchanging a hug and condolences with her. Claire said, "I am so sorry for your loss, Marie. I don't know if you remember me. I'm Claire Boswell. My mother lived on the reserve before she married my father."

"Of course I remember you, dear. And I know you helped discover her body." She stopped talking, choking up. "Oh, what's the world coming to?" she sobbed.

"Have the police found out what happened to her?"

"I don't know. The community engagement officer can't tell me, and I never saw the policemen who came up from Fort McMurray. I blame myself. I should never have let her go out in the evening. But you know how kids are at that age! It hasn't been easy raising her by myself. She stopped going to high school when she was sixteen, and she was very independent."

"Was she seeing someone? Did she have a boyfriend?"

"I don't know, I don't know!" Marie broke down in tears. After a few moments, she calmed down and wiped her eyes. "Sadie is one person who she saw a lot of, a girl on the reserve. She might know other people she hung out with."

Claire gave her a hug. "I'll try to find out for you." She rejoined Beth, who was talking to Migizi. "I wasn't able to learn much from her mother. I think we need to go to speak to people at the mine where she was found."

Migizi looked sceptical. "They're going to refuse to talk to you. I can't even set foot on the land where the mine is located. They do what they want there, they're not accountable to the Fort McKay First Nation."

Claire stuck out her chin. "We'll see."

*****

Claire and Beth drove up to the main gate of the mine where Beverly Racette's body was found, followed by Migizi driving the Peace Officer cruiser. They pulled up to the guard house. A man wearing a uniform came out and walked to the driver's side. He asked Claire politely, "What is your business at the mine?"

"We'd like to talk to a supervisor about the body which was found on the mine site, Beverly Racette. She was buried at the Fort McKay cemetery today. Her mother wants to know what happened."

"I'm sorry, the matter is out of our hands. It's the responsibility of the RCMP."

"We'd still like to talk to the people who discovered her body."

"There's nobody here who can talk to you. Perhaps you want to speak with our press office in Calgary? Otherwise, try the RCMP in Fort McMurray." The guard looked at Migizi, who had stayed in his cruiser. "What are you doing here? No unauthorized access." He turned away. Since the gate was closed, they had no choice but to turn around.

Claire said to Beth, "Let's stop at The Lodge and decide what we should do next." She motioned to Migizi to follow her into the lodge's parking lot. He got out and joined them in her car, sitting in the back seat.

"We can't let it go," Claire said. "There must be a way of getting in to look around. I know from the drone video at least where she was found. I want to see if there are any clues. Migizi, are there any breaks in the fence?"

"Not that I know of. And even if you got in, it's all open ground. There's no place to hide. You'd be spotted in no time."

Beth spoke up. "I know what we could do! You could ask George to smuggle us in, and he can take us in his truck to the place where Beverly was found!"

Migizi shook his head. "Too risky. And he'd be fired if they found out."

Beth was undeterred. "Why don't you call him, Claire, and see what he says?"

George agreed to take Claire and Beth into the Muskeg River Mine complex the next day, when his shift started. "I'll pick you up at 10 am at The Lodge. Wear dark clothing if you have some, and boots. You're going to get dirty."

Claire and Beth headed back to Fort McMurray to put together what they needed for the next day. They were both in a serious mood. "Beth, why don't you come over to my father's house for dinner, we can plan out what we should do tomorrow?"

"OK, sure, that's a good idea."

26

Fort McKay

The morning was cloudy and windy, with a chance of rain later, when Claire and Beth set off once again for Fort McKay. They wore jeans and windbreakers which had already been well used. On their feet were old work boots. Beth had borrowed clothes from Claire's father, since Claire's were too small for her. Claire carried a rucksack with her camera equipment.

A little before ten, George drove up in an old pick-up truck and parked next to them at The Lodge. "You'll have to climb into the back and get under the tarp. We can't have anyone see you. Get in!"

The guard at the gate waved George through, and he wound his way around a mass of buildings housing administration and maintenance facilities, and past vast tanks for storing oil, water, and solvents. A monstrous upgrading plant in the distance belched steam and smoke. The ambient noise continually assaulted their ears. George stopped at a hangar containing the huge trucks that were used to take the bitumen scooped up by giant mechanical shovels to the plant.

He got out. Standing by the pickup's bed, he said, "Don't come out yet. I'll check if there's anyone else around. If not, then you can follow me to the Cat and climb up to the cab."

After five minutes, he returned, and said in a low voice, "Come with me, quickly!"

When Beth saw the Caterpillar 797F, the 400 tonne hauler, she gasped. "It's so enormous!"

George hurried the two women along. "We'll have to climb up all those rungs to get to the cab. Let's do it, now!"

At the top, twenty feet off the ground, George motioned for them to hide in a corner of the cab while he started the truck and drove out of the hangar. They had shown him where on a drone photo the body was found. "I can take you there, but you'll have to get down from the truck quickly. I can't stop there for more than a few seconds. If I do, I may get stuck in the bitumen. I'll come back for you on my way to the upgrading plant, when my truck is loaded."

The truck left the area where the buildings were and took a road through the oil sands that had already been mined. Enormous scars marked the landscape. The truck raised clouds of dust as it made its way over the unpaved road. The noise from the engine was deafening. As they approached the tailings pond George motioned for them to start down the ladder. He stopped where the road neared the water, and Claire and Beth scurried down the rest of the ladder, dropping from the last rung to the ground. George continued on his way.

It was sticky underfoot. According to George, the ideal temperature for mining was -10 C. Otherwise, the sand mixed with bitumen could be soft and slippery, as it was today. The road where George had driven was scored by the tread marks from many large tires. The land beside it was bare. It was devoid of vegetation but exhibited tracks left by the giant scoops that had mined the bitumen months before.

Claire looked back the way they had come. "At least there's a hill that shelters us from view of the buildings." She pointed ahead to the tailings pond. "This is where her body was visible on the video."

The water was oily, and it had a chemical smell. There was a dead bird in the water, its feathers soaked in the black liquid. They followed the shoreline until they came to some footprints. "It's probably where they pulled out the body." Claire took photos.

They looked around for other evidence of recent human contact, walking in increasing arcs. "There!" Beth said, pointing to a scratch in the soil. "I'll bet her body was dragged from that direction." She looked toward the haulage road. "Let's see if we can find something up there."

The ground was soft underfoot, and it was slow going to climb the hill. Just before reaching the road, they found a small purse lying on the ground, half buried in the oil sand. Claire took a picture. Gently inserting it into a ziploc bag, she stored it in her rucksack.

At the roadside, a set of car tire prints was visible in the bitumen–strikingly smaller than those made by the hauling trucks. "I'll bet whoever dumped Beverly's body made these. I'll take pics. They were recently made."

They saw a big Cat approaching along the road. Claire said, "I hope it's George, but I can't tell from here." They moved back, because the truck spanned the roadway. "No, it's not George!" The truck continued past, the driver looking curiously down at them. He was talking into a mobile communications device.

"Let's get the hell out of here," Beth said. "They're onto us!" She started up the hill toward the fence that guarded the perimeter. The ground was soft, and each step was a struggle because of the stickiness of the bitumen. They were three-quarters of the way to the fence when Claire looked behind and saw a jeep approaching along the road from the main complex. "Run," she said. "If we can make it to the fence we'll be harder to spot."

Beth got there first, ducking down next to the fence. It was anchored by posts made of concrete. The chain-link was ten feet high. Above it was a dog-leg of barbed wire, supported by angled struts attached to the concrete posts. "Come on!" she yelled.

Claire finally made it to the fence, and Beth pulled her down to ground level. There was just enough of a berm so that they were below the jeep's line-of-sight. They rested there, panting, while watching the top of the vehicle continue towards the place near the tailings pond where they had been a few minutes before.

The fence paralleled the access road from which they had entered the main gate. They crept along it in the direction of highway 63 and away from the gate at the entrance to the mine. "If only we could find a place to squeeze through!" Claire said, despair in her voice. The fence was solidly attached to the posts, and there was no way to climb over it. Looking back toward the tailings pond, they saw that the jeep had stopped near to where they had been passed by the big Cat. They knelt down in front of a post and waited.

Looking around her desperately, Claire noticed that an animal seemed to have dug a hole under the fence. She pointed to it. "If we can enlarge it a little, we can get out that way. We've got to find a stick or a rock! Wait! I see something on the other side. I'm smaller than you. I'll try to reach it from under the fence."

Claire handed Beth her rucksack, scraped some of the soil away using her hands, and wedged her body under the fence. "No, I can't go any further. I'll see if I can stretch and grab whatever it is." In another minute she said, "Pull me out!" Beth grabbed her feet and tugged her out of the hole. Claire had tar on her face, but she triumphantly held up a large paint can with a metal top, trash that had blown against the outside of the fence.

Claire dug while Beth pushed the soil away from the opening. Soon, the hole was large enough for Claire to try again. The jeep had turned around, and was approaching. She wriggled under the fence, but her windbreaker caught on a wire link at the bottom when she was halfway through. She couldn't move her arms to get at it. "Beth! I'm stuck. Reach forward and free me!" Beth knelt next to the hole and scrabbled at the material. At last, Claire slithered her way through. "Now, pass me my rucksack and one of the scoops so I can enlarge this side. You do the same on your side!"

After another minute Beth decided to give it a try. Sliding into the hole, she managed to get her head clear of the fence and was wriggling her body forward. Then she could go no further. "You've got to pull me! Take my arms." She stretched them out in front of her.

Claire saw that the jeep had left the road and was advancing cautiously in their direction. There were two men in it. She grabbed Beth's hands and pulled backwards with all her strength. At first, Beth wouldn't budge. Then little by little she inched forward, helped by the greasy consistency of the bitumen. At last her legs cleared the chain links at the bottom of the fence. Allowing themselves no time to catch their breaths, they ran toward The Lodge, which was some 500 metres away. In another few minutes, they made it to the parking lot where Claire had left her car. She fumbled for her keys in a panic. *Where are they, where are they?* Finally, she located them in her rucksack. She unlocked the doors, and they threw themselves into the car. After two tries the engine started. Claire put it into Drive and drove away quickly from the parking lot. She checked the access road for other vehicles. *None in sight!* She peeled out onto the road, while staring in her rear-view mirror to make sure she wasn't followed.

"Phew, that was close," Beth said. "We have a head start on that jeep, which has to go back out the gate. So floor it. Once we're on the highway I think we're safe. They don't know what car you're driving."

Claire and Beth did a fist bump after turning south onto 63, both of them visibly more relaxed now. Claire asked Beth to call George to tell him not to worry. "I don't want him to start looking for us. If he does, they'll suspect that we entered the site in his pickup truck. I'm sure by now they've discovered the hole under the fence. I'd like them to think that we came in that way."

George picked up after five rings. "Oh, it's you! There's a jeep parked beside the fence, and someone is poking around there. Is that where you got out? Are the two of you OK?"

"Yes, we're fine George. They don't suspect you, do they?"

"Not so far. I'll complete my shift, then take off to the reserve as soon as I can."

27

Fort McMurray

Once back at Claire's father's place the two women looked through the purse they had found at the mine. It had several compartments, for IDs, credit cards, cash, and coins. It contained a few dollars and a driver's licence in the name of Beverly Racette. Beth asked herself why the purse hadn't been found before. "Obviously, the RCMP's investigation wasn't very thorough. They seem to have known that the woman was Beverly, in any case. I wonder how."

Claire nodded. "Even more disturbing is the RCMP doesn't seem to have spotted the tire marks at the spot where her body was offloaded from a car and dragged to the tailings pond. It's as if they hadn't looked and didn't care."

Tom came in the door with a bag of groceries, took one look at the two creatures covered with tar, and let out a mock "eek!" before pretending to head out the door. "While I make dinner, you two ladies are going to have to do a lot of scrubbing!"

Beth nodded her agreement. "I'll go back to my hotel and take a long shower, then change into something that's not stained with bitumen. Give me an hour and I'll be back here. I'm famished."

"You can just throw away those clothes I lent you," Tom said. "They're not worth trying to wash the tar out."

Beth walked back to the hotel, which was only a few minutes away. It was after five o'clock. Shops were closing and people were going home from work. As she crossed the lobby of the hotel to take the elevator, she spotted Flora sitting in one of the armchairs.

"What are you doing here? Is everything OK?"

"Can we talk? I have some news I picked up at work."

"Sure, why don't you come up to my room? I'll tell you what Claire and I were doing today, and why I look like I've been wrestling with the tar baby!"

When they reached Beth's room, she motioned Flora to take a seat as she removed her stained jacket and boots, which she threw into a waste basket. "Fire away," she said.

"I think I know where the guards went. They're not *desaparecidos*, they were actually transferred to another job site by WOS. They're now security guards at the Syncrude oil sands mine site at Mildred Lake, between here and Fort McKay."

"That's good to know, because Claire and I have found out some more things in Fort McKay about the death of that indigenous girl, Beverly. We were smuggled into the mine site by a friend of Claire's who drives a haulage truck. We picked up Beverly's purse, and took pics of the tire prints of a car located near to where she was dumped. Then we were spotted, and we ended up crawling under the perimeter fence to get away."

"Wow, you have had *un dia muy interesante!*"

"Tell me, Flora, does WOS have another office in Mildred Lake, or are the security guards still the responsibility of your Fort McMurray office? Can you find out where they live? And is it usual to have them rotate between job sites?"

"I've never met them, they were living at The Lodge up in Fort McKay when they were working there. I expect there's a similar set up for them now in Mildred Lake. Because their housing is arranged by the company they change locations as needed. But we don't have another office there. It's just them. They swapped places with two of our guys who are now working at the Muskeg River Mine in Fort McKay."

"And in this case, they got a new assignment in order to get them out of the firing line, so to speak?"

"*Si,* you got it."

"Can you find out their names and exactly where they live?"

"I'll do my best."

✳✳✳✳✳

Beth, Claire, and Tom were sitting around the kitchen table eating spaghetti bolognese that Tom had made when Claire's phone rang. Speaking rapidly, George said, "I can't talk long but I wanted to let you know that Beverly was definitely seeing one of the security guards, Jeff Stevens. One of the other haulage drivers noticed her with him in the security van last week. He's not sure of the day, but it was close to the time you spotted her body on the drone video. Stevens must have smuggled her in.

I'm at the mine site now, about to card out. Talk again soon." He ended the call.

Claire turned to Beth. "We need to track down those security guards, in particular Jeff Stevens. How do we do that?"

"Flora is going to try to find out where they are exactly. She says that they're still working for WOS, but as guards at the Mildred Lake site. We're not going to be able to get access to the work site, so we need to catch them at home. When she finds out where they live we'll try to talk to them."

*****

It was late morning on Saturday, and Beth hoped to find Jeff Stevens at the suites hotel in the north end of Fort McMurray. Flora had sneaked a look at the employee records and found where he lived now. Since Mildred Lake was close to Fort McMurray, WOS had decided to house them there.

The receptionist consulted her directory. "He's in 221B. Take the elevator to the second floor and turn right when you get off."

An unshaven man in his thirties answered the knock, opening the door the few centimetres that the chain would allow. Beth hadn't seen the guard very well who had tried to take the drone video from them in Fort McKay, but he seemed familiar.

The man looked puzzled, then he noticed the attractive woman at his door. He gave Beth a smarmy smile. "Hello! What can I do for you?"

"I'm collecting for the United Way. Would you like to make a donation?"

"Uh, sorry, no. I've just moved here, and I've got a lot of expenses."

"Oh, that's too bad. Where have you come from?"

"Up north. I work for an oil services company."

Beth smiled at him. "That's very interesting. What do you do?"

He shuffled his feet. "I'm a security guard, actually. But my job comes with a car." He looked at her hopefully.

Beth put on her most earnest expression. "Great! Maybe we could go someplace together then. How about driving to Edmonton to do some shopping? Are you free today?"

He looked uncertain. "I'd have to check with my roommate. And we're not supposed to use the company car for long trips. They check the odometer every month when we submit our expenses for gas and such. My roommate has his own car but it's not in very good shape. So I guess we're grounded."

"Oh, too bad! Maybe we'll meet some other time, then."

Another head emerged from around the door. "Hi there, I'm Al. Do you have a car? Maybe we could go with you to Edmonton?"

Beth shuffled her feet. "Actually, my car needs to go into the garage for some work. It wouldn't get us to Edmonton and back!" She nodded goodbye to them and headed back down the hall.

Beth returned to her rental car and told Claire that the security van was probably in the parking garage at the back of the building. "Let's have a quick look to see if the tires match the treads we photographed at the Muskeg River Mine."

They walked up the ramp to the garage and looked around. As expected, there was a small yellow van with "Wildcat Oil Services" marked on both sides. Claire used her phone's camera to take pictures of the treads on the front and back tires. "Hopefully this will be enough to identify the van as the one that Beverly was seen in."

As they were leaving Beth spotted Jeff Stevens opening the door from the suites to the garage, accompanied by Al. *Uh-oh,* she thought. She averted her gaze and said to Claire, "Quick, let's get out of here." They hurried out of the garage and around to the front of the building, got into Claire's car, and were driving away by the time the WOS van pulled out of the garage.

*****

Beth downloaded the photos taken at the mine and those Claire had taken of the van's tires into a photo editing app. Zooming in on both and viewing them side by side confirmed that it was the same vehicle. "We've got enough to start talking turkey to that turkey at the RCMP," Beth said to Claire with a laugh.

"You're right. There's not much we can do about it ourselves except keep the pressure on them to look into Beverly's death."

Beth gritted her teeth. "We need those bastards to do a serious job of investigating what happened to her. We can't let them ignore another suspicious death of an indigenous woman! We need to talk to someone more senior than Constable Brown."

*****

On Monday morning they drove to the RCMP detachment office. The same receptionist was at her post inside the main entrance. Beth strode up to her. "Last week we spoke to Constable Brown about the death of a young woman, Beverly Racette, in Fort McKay. We have new evidence that someone was seen with her shortly before her death. She was riding in his van close to the place her body was found. We would like to speak to Constable Brown's supervisor about this."

"I'll check to see if Constable Brown is available."

"No, we want to talk to his supervisor," Beth said firmly.

"Why is that?"

"Constable Brown made it quite clear that he was not serious about investigating her death and that he had no interest in talking to us. This is a serious matter and we want our evidence to be given serious attention."

"I'll see what I can do."

They waited for 20 minutes, first standing up, then, after 10 minutes, sitting on an uncomfortable bench. Finally, a tall man with grey hair who was walking with a limp came over to them. "I'm Inspector St. James. I was told that you had some new evidence in the Beverly Racette case? Can you show me what it is?"

Beth said, "It would help if we can display it on your computer's screen. We have some photos."

The man sighed. "Very well. I'll take you to a conference room." He led them to a room at the back of the building, which had a projector hooked up to a computer. "Now explain to me what you have. I can't spare a lot of time on this." He looked ostentatiously at his watch.

Claire broke in. "This is an important matter. A woman died, and so far the RCMP has shown little interest in finding out what happened. If you persist, we're going to the media."

St. James raised his eyebrows. "And the evidence you have?"

Claire continued, "We're the ones who spotted the body with a drone, which we reported to the police. In the face of your inaction in investigating her death, we searched the site where her body was located. We found her purse, as well as the tire tracks of a vehicle–the only ones not made by the gigantic haulers they use to carry the bitumen. We can show you a photo of the tracks."

"OK, let's put them up on the screen. You'll need to give me precise details of where and when they were taken. But what does that tell us? How do we know that Beverly was in the vehicle?"

Claire responded, "I've obtained the testimony of someone I know that Beverly was seen at the mine with one of the security guards, Jeff Stevens. They were sitting in his van. Not coincidentally, the guard and his partner have been transferred away from the Fort McKay mine by Wildcat Oil Services."

"Where are they now? Do you know?"

Beth answered triumphantly, "We've located that same security van, which those guards are using at their current job at the Mildred Lake site. The tire treads match those we discovered at the Muskeg River Mine where they used to work. Here's a memory stick with the two sets of photos."

Looking dubious, St. James said, "Let me put them up on the screen to have a look. Hmm, I see. They do seem to be identical, but I would need to document when and where they were taken before proceeding any further."

"The photos do have a time stamp, and it's clear from the first one where they were taken on the mine site. I can give you the address where the van is now parked, and you can verify it for yourself!"

"But surely it's no surprise that the security van's tread marks were found at the Fort McKay mine, since it was their job to patrol the site? And just because the girl was in their van doesn't provide any basis for concluding that one of them murdered her, does it?"

Beth responded, "The evidence throws a strong suspicion on them, one that should be investigated! Surely the body should have been examined for any DNA linking her to a possible assailant. Has the Force determined how she died? Any traces of DNA on her body could now be matched with that from the two security guards. And the van could similarly be examined for any traces that she might have left there."

"Very well, I will take this up with Constable Brown. Give me also the name of the person who saw her in the van at the mine, and turn over any evidence you picked up at the site. I should emphasize that you had no business sneaking into the mine and interfering with what may indeed be a crime site. Moreover, you seem to have appointed yourselves private investigators. Am I right to think that you're not licensed to do that job here in Alberta?" He glared at Beth.

She glared back at him. "We're not doing this for a client. We're only acting as private citizens to ensure that justice is done!"

St. James left the discussion there, and escorted the two women back to the lobby.

On the way back to the car, Beth said, "I'll give them 36 hours, and if there's nothing on the news, I'll go public with the information we have."

"Amen, sister!"

28

The newscaster was giving his news summary on a local Edmonton television station. "Our reporter in Fort Mc-Murray has just attended a press conference given by two women who have been investigating the death of a Fort McKay indigenous woman, Beverly Racette. What did you hear, Mary Jane?"

"Thanks, Wilt. The two women, Claire Boswell and Beth Phillips, accuse the RCMP of incompetence in investigating her death and indifference to the plight of indigenous women. They were the ones who located the body of Beverly Racette, who had been reported missing by her mother, using footage from a drone. In the absence of an RCMP response they travelled to the place where her body was found, which was a tailings pond at the Muskeg River Mine in Fort McKay. They gathered testimony from someone who works at the mine that Beverly was seen in the vehicle driven by a security guard from Wildcat Oil Services shortly before she died. Since the RCMP has shown no interest in the case, the two women are appealing to the general public for any information and to the perpetrator or perpetrators of what looks like a murder to surrender to the police."

Beth and Claire were watching the news in the lobby of the Pomeroy Hotel. Beth said, "That should set the cat among the pigeons! Let's see what the RCMP does now."

*****

The tall police officer first knocked on the door of the AOSCP trailer and then opened it. Sarah looked up, startled. "What is it that you want?"

"I'm Inspector St. James. I'm looking for Claire Boswell. Do you know where she is?"

"Why should I tell you? I expect you just want to harass her."

St. James was taken aback by her answer. "Now wait a minute! You've got this all wrong. I just wanted to consult her about Beverly Racette's death, her and her friend Beth Phillips."

"Oh, and I'm supposed to believe that, given your past lack of interest in the case?"

"We've decided to go all-in on the investigation. The top brass of the RCMP wants this to be settled, wherever the chips may fall. So we need all the information we can get. Please ask them to get in touch with me. Here's my card. They can use my direct line to call me."

"Tell you what, I'll pass on your message to them. They can decide what to do next, whether they want to get back to you."

*****

"Beverly's friend Sadie came to see me at the First Nations office," Migizi told Claire over the phone. "She thinks Beverly might have been killed because she views the oil sands mining as a form of ecocide. She and Beverly were gathering incriminating information about the oil companies' operations."

"Whoa, back up! Are you saying she was inside the Muskeg River Mine not because of some romantic encounter but because she was spying on them?"

"Sadie said that the two of them and another girl were aiming to 'name and shame' the oil companies that stripped the forests, polluted the atmosphere, and fouled the rivers–including the Muskeg River. They admire what Greta Thunberg has been doing to focus attention on global warming, and want to do something similar about the environmental damage and emissions from mining the oil sands. Sadie thinks that Beverly somehow got someone to smuggle her into the mine, or managed to sneak in on her own, so she could make the public aware of the environmental disaster. She was planning to take pictures. They may have gotten her killed."

"How are we going to prove this? Does Sadie have any evidence?"

"Unfortunately not."

"Migizi, would you ask Beverly's mother if she would mind if we looked through her daughter's things at their home? They might yield some clues. I could come up to Fort McKay and the two of us could examine them. "

*****

Marie Racette lived in a trailer on the reserve, not far from the First Nation's administration building. "Come on in, you two. You can look through her things. I sorted some of them out, but I don't know what to look for."

"You take the bedroom, and I'll go through the closet at the back of the trailer," Migizi said to Claire.

Marie showed Claire where Beverly's bedroom was. "You know, I think Migizi is sweet on you!" She giggled. "Anyway, there are term papers and notes in the dresser. Why don't you start there?"

Claire removed several notebooks filled with handwritten information about Beverly's coursework. They dated back to two years previously. She flipped through them, and saw that there were numerous references to the history and geography of the region. She turned to Beverly's mother. "She seemed to have taken quite an interest in the First Nation."

"She sure did. That was her favourite course. Too bad she didn't want to stay in school. She never got a high school diploma. She thought it was more important to do something for her community. That's why she was so determined to find out what was going on with the oil sands."

At the bottom of the drawer was a bound volume, a sort of ledger that an accountant might use. Claire leafed through it. On one page there was a list of spills of chemicals and reports of contaminations of rivers and lakes, and the dates they occurred. On another, a record of the demise of members of the First Nation, with annotations concerning the cause of death. A third section reported on the number of animals found in their traps by hunters. A graph plotted their downward trend. On the back page was a list of organizations campaigning against environmental destruction, global warming. and the use of fossil fuels. The list included AOSCP, the NGO where Claire worked.

"Beverly seemed to be doing some serious research. Do you know what she intended to do with this?"

"I heard her and Sadie saying that they would start by writing an article for our local news-sheet here, and then try to interest the regional media. They were determined to alert Albertans to the evils of oil sands development."

"It's too bad she didn't join our NGO, which is doing exactly what you said she wanted."

"She said that the local organizations she knew about didn't go far enough. They were all talk and no action."

Migizi emerged from the back room. "The only thing I found of interest were some clippings of photographs of oil sands mining sites and of the equipment the oil companies use to dig up and process the sands. There's nothing that indicates what they intended to do with them. Do you know, Marie?"

"Sadie might know. You could call her. I'll give you her phone number."

"I don't want to discuss this on the phone," Sadie said to Claire, when she called. "I need to visit Fort McMurray tomorrow anyway. Why don't I stop by where you work? Can you give me the address?"

*****

Sadie came the next day to the AOSCP trailer to speak to Claire and Beth. She was an intense and serious-looking young woman who could not disguise the anger she felt against those who were destroying her homeland. An elastic band gathered her long black hair together, whose ends hung down her back. She was dressed in jeans and a sweatshirt inscribed with "Fort McKay First Nation" in both English and Dene.

Sadie explained what she and Beverly had been doing. "We were pulling together evidence that the oil companies are committing ecocide hand in glove with the government of Alberta. We've got to make our fellow citizens sit up and listen! They're so ignorant! In case you don't know, ecocide is the wanton and large-scale destruction of the environment. You realize that a number of countries consider that a crime against humanity? Not Canada, though. We're too addicted to making money out of the black gold under the earth's surface."

Claire and Beth were sitting opposite to her in the NGO's trailer. Beth shook her head. "You don't have to convince us! We're on your side! We're trying to figure out if her crusade against the oil sands got her killed. Can you tell us why and how she was able to get inside the mine site?"

"We were talking about how to get pictures of the Muskeg River Mine. They don't want anyone to photograph the site, so we needed to trick our way past the gate. Beverly figured that she could chat up someone who works there to take her in, and then she would be able to take pics with her cell phone. We were going to visit The Lodge together and talk to some of the workers who hang out there. But my mother found out about it and grounded me. So Beverly went alone. I don't know what happened to her. I should have been there to protect her!" She bowed her head and tears glistened on her cheeks.

Claire put her arm around Sadie's shoulders. "Don't blame yourself. It's not your fault. Did you know any of the security guards personally? Had Beverly ever talked to one of them before?"

"We went to The Lodge a few times, though we weren't supposed to. I think she might have met one of them earlier, but I'm not sure."

"We're trying to get the RCMP to investigate her death and find out what happened," Beth said to her. She gave Sadie a hug. "I think you should go talk to the Inspector in charge, St. James."

Sadie shook her head. "No, definitely not! I don't want to do that!"

"Why not?"

She hesitated. "Because I might get into trouble! Beverly and I were talking about doing more than just writing articles. We read about people like Gandhi, how he used civil disobedience to advance his cause. I contacted some of the other ecology groups to see what they could do to help us. Our idea was to disrupt the operations of the mine, do a sit-in to prevent the trucks from getting by–that sort of thing. Maybe even slashing their tires. So I don't want to be questioned by the RCMP!"

Claire said, "I can understand that. How far did you get in your planning? Did you tell anyone else about it on the reserve?"

"No, we were just tossing around ideas among ourselves–me, Beverly, and Lydia–a friend of ours. The other groups we contacted were enthusiastic but they're not located here so they couldn't commit to doing anything concrete."

Beth looked puzzled. She turned to Claire. "No one has mentioned finding her cell phone. That might be an important clue that reveals what actually happened to Beverly. It's something that we need to ask the RCMP about."

29

Inspector St. James invited Beth and Claire into his office at the RCMP detachment building in Fort McMurray. His manner was much more welcoming than at their previous meeting. "I must apologize to you for my tepid reaction to the information you brought me. You're quite right, the RCMP did not treat this case with the seriousness that it deserves. I would like you to sit in on a meeting I am calling with my staff assigned to the case. You'll see that now we mean business."

He led them to a conference room nearby, where two men were sitting around the table. "You've met Constable Brown. This is Sergeant Reynaldo."

St. James explained to them that the two women would be helping their investigation. "Since you two couldn't get to the bottom of this, I brought in some assistance," he said in a sardonic tone. "These are the women who discovered the body, came up with the name of a security guard who was seen with Beverly Racette shortly before she died, and located him after he had been transferred to another job by Wildcat Oil Services." The two police officers looked contrite.

Beth said, "We believe that Jeff Stevens, perhaps with the connivance of his partner, drove Beverly into the Muskeg

River Mine complex. It's unclear whose idea this was, Beverly's or Jeff's. In any case, it would have been easy for her to hide in the van when they entered by the main gate. There are plenty of buildings on site that they could have used as a hideout. What happened then I don't know. Perhaps it was an accident, or perhaps it was murder. It is up to the RCMP to investigate her cause of death. I believe that one or both men then dumped her body in the tailings pond. I suspect that they thought it would sink below the surface and be hidden among the scum in the water. Perhaps the gas from decomposition of the body made it float to the surface."

St. James glared at his underlings. "We're going to have to exhume the body. You should at least have determined the cause of death!" He turned back to the two women. "What makes you suspect the security guards, aside from the testimony of the hauler driver–I think you said George was his name–who saw Beverly in their van?"

Claire replied. "We were surprised that a guard would shoot down our drone, and try to force us to give them the video footage. They were unnecessarily aggressive. That made us go back to look at the site. Then George told us about Beverly being seen with one of the guards. Furthermore, a friend of Beverly's suggested to us that she wanted to get inside the mine complex in order to take pictures, and was going to try to chat up one of the workers to get her through the gate. This provided a possible reason why Beverly was in the WOS van."

"Hmm. So you suspected one of the guards. How did you find them here in Fort McMurray? You said that you thought that they had been transferred from Fort McKay or told to disappear so that they couldn't be questioned."

Beth hesitated before answering. "We have a source at WOS who gave us this information. We can't reveal that person's name. Doing so might endanger the source's life."

"Very well. But we're going to need to question the personnel at WOS in any case to find out what they know."

"Then you have to ask them why WOS is covering up for the security guards. Was the boss of the Fort McMurray office made aware that a crime had been committed in Fort McKay? If so, surely that makes him an accomplice?"

St. James shook his head. "I think you're getting ahead of yourself. Let's start by talking to the WOS's manager." Turning to Beth, he said, "It might be helpful for you to be there too."

"Happy to! There's another important unresolved issue: where is Beverly's phone? Did she take the pictures that were the reason she wanted to go there in the first place? Someone needs to find it."

St. James turned to his minions. "Organize a more thorough search of the area where the woman was found to see if you can locate the cell phone and anything else that might be relevant. A careful search should have been done at the time the body was removed. You even missed her purse, which was lying on the ground! If the phone doesn't turn up there, then we will have to search the buildings at the mine and the lodgings of the security guards."

*****

"News at Noon has learned that two Fort McMurray men are being sought by the police investigating the death of an indigenous woman in Fort McKay, Beverly Racette. What do we know about that, Mary Jane?"

"Yes, thank you Wilt. The RCMP have just finished a media briefing. Her death is now considered to be due to foul play. Two Wildcat Oil Services security guards who used to patrol the Muskeg River oil sands site in Fort McKay are considered to be 'persons of interest' and are being actively sought. The Force could not give us details at the moment, though Inspector St. James promises to hold another briefing soon. He assures us that the RCMP are giving their utmost attention to solving this case."

30

"How long have you been the WOS manager here in Fort McMurray, Mr. Thomas?" asked St. James, who was sitting in the man's office. He was accompanied by Beth, and had introduced her as a civilian who was helping with the investigation. Howard Thomas was a slender man wearing slacks and a polo neck shirt who appeared to be in his forties.

"I moved here three years ago. Before that, I was the manager at our Peace River office."

"And how long have you been with the company?"

"From the beginning, actually. I grew up with Ruben Gallant in Nova Scotia–he's the president of the company–and we both moved out to Alberta in the early 1990s. We stayed in touch, though Ruben was doing back office work and I was at the wellhead. After various jobs in different places out here, we got together and decided to form a company, found some backers, including a venture capital company back home, and in the early 2000s Wildcat Oil Services was born. Ruben became president and I've set up various offices throughout the province. I like to be close to the action."

"And the 'action' is what, exactly?"

"We do anything needed to support the industry. The oil sands are the greatest opportunity Canada has ever had–bigger than the fur trade, bigger than the gold mines, bigger than all the Prairie wheat. We help the industry mine the oil sands, upgrade and ship its oil, and sell it to US refineries. Just think of it: thanks in large part to the oil sands, Canada produces 5 million barrels of oil per day, much of it exported. It has the fourth largest oil reserves in the world. If Canada turned its back on this godsend, we'd be paupers."

"And what does this office do to service the oil sands?"

"We provide security, environmental assessments, and assistance with planning the oil extraction operations, both mining and *in situ* extraction."

Beth interrupted. "It's security we would like to talk about. You have personnel at various mine sites here. What do they do, and how are they assigned to one place rather than another? And security against what, exactly?"

Thomas paused to formulate an answer. "The guards are posted at the sites to protect the public. Our earth moving equipment is massive. You wouldn't believe how big our haulers are: they have a 400 tonne capacity! The plants that generate superheated steam to inject into the bitumen deposits to separate the bitumen from the sand and those that upgrade the heavy oil are no places for tourists! We can't allow any public access. It's too dangerous."

"Actually, I've seen the big haulers, and even ridden in one," Beth said dryly. "You're right, they are frightening. But the oil sands sites are protected by high fences. Isn't that enough?"

He hesitated before replying to her question. "We hope so, but it's good to have backup. At least the oil companies think so."

"Isn't it also to keep out people with prying eyes, who might generate unfavourable publicity? Don't you forbid your personnel from taking pictures of the sites, and try to prevent others from doing so?"

"Well, I …. I guess that's one interpretation. But our goal is just to ensure the safe exploitation of the oil sands."

St. James resumed his control of the questioning. "We understand that two WOS security guards at the Muskeg River Mine left recently. One of those guards was seen on site with an indigenous girl, barely 18, shortly before she died. She was later found floating in a tailings pond," he turned and nodded at Beth, "by someone flying a drone over the site. We would like to know where we can find those guards. Are they still working for WOS?"

"Why yes, they are currently patrolling the Syncrude Mildred Lake site."

"How did it happen that they left MRM so suddenly?"

Thomas started to look worried. He stammered, "We rotate our guards periodically. It keeps them sharp, and prevents them from getting too close to people who might lull them into a false complacency and lead them to let their guard down."

"Really? And how long were they in their position at Muskeg River?"

"It was, let me see, about three months," he said lamely.

"So it was just a routine rotation? I understand that they exchanged places with the guards who had been at Mildred Lake for a year."

Thomas looked toward the door, like a cornered rat. "I … I'd have to check my records, but that might be true. Yes, it was just a routine rotation."

The Inspector's phone rang. He looked at it and said, "I'd better take that."

St. James stood up. "That's all for now. But you might want to reconsider your position on that point. I'll return after we've spoken to some of your staff." He stepped outside, saying into his phone, "Go ahead, give me the results."

St. James huddled with Beth in the parking lot of the WOS building. "The autopsy showed an injury to Beverly's head, but also found water in her lungs. She died from drowning. These developments are going to make it even more urgent to solve the case. I'm being summoned to Divisional HQ in Edmonton to give a briefing, so I'm not going to be able to interview WOS staff. I'm leaving Constable Brown to follow up with the questioning."

"He and I are not on the same page. I don't think he'll want me involved, so I'll bow out, at least for now."

"As you wish."

*****

"Flora, what do you say we meet with Claire tonight?" Beth said softly. She had gone back into the WOS office before leaving for her hotel. Constable Brown was hovering at the entrance. He hadn't acknowledged her presence when he arrived. He had merely requested to see the staff in order to ask them a few questions. They were assembling in a conference room nearby.

Flora nodded. "See you there," she whispered. She got up and joined the other staff.

*****

Beth, Claire, and Flora sat in Tom's cramped living room, furnished with a few ageing armchairs and a sofa which didn't match. "Tell us, Flora, what happened with Constable Brown this afternoon," Beth asked.

"*Nada.* He just asked for the personnel records of Stevens and his partner Al Marino, wanted to know if anyone else from WOS knew them, and asked us to contact him if we come across information about their activities in Fort McKay. But you know, I'm sure I've seen this constable before talking to our boss, Mr. Thomas. It was the day you went up to Fort McKay the first time, to interview someone up there and you took the video of the tailings pond."

"Oh yeah? What were they talking about?"

"I dunno, but it seemed pretty heavy stuff, since the boss was shaking his head and looking worried. As I told you before, I thought there was someone from the RCMP who came to talk to the boss, and that's why the guards were transferred. I didn't know who it was, but now I do. It was Brown."

Claire shook her head. "Brown must somehow have known what happened to Beverly by then–way earlier than what we were told before, and before we spotted her body on the drone video. You've got to talk to St. James about this and get to the bottom of it."

*****

Migizi, the Fort McKay First Nations Peace Officer, called Claire. "I don't know if this is important, but I was looking through the log book for the last few weeks and I came across an entry that mentions Constable Brown. He came up to Fort McKay from Fort McMurray and was asking about Beverly."

"Why is that surprising?"

"Well, normally someone from the RCMP is not going to waste his or her time coming up to Fort McKay just to investigate a missing person's report. That's why I was curious about this entry. Then when I looked at the date, I realized that Brown's visit occurred before she was actually reported missing by her mother."

"Any idea what he was asking about?"

"Nope. He never came to see me."

"Could you ask around to see who he might have talked to and what it was about?"

"OK, I'll do my best."

*****

Migizi called Claire back the next day. "I talked to Beverly's mother, and she told me something she hadn't mentioned before that jibes with what Sadie said. Beverly was involved with other young people on the reserve who were violently opposed to the oil sands development. They might have been trying to sabotage the mine in some way."

"Wow! So maybe she was using Jeff Stevens to smuggle her through the gate. When he got heavy with her, she freaked out and tried to run away. But they would have to be in cahoots. She would need to carry something with her in order to sabotage the mine–explosives or cable cutters or something. She couldn't very well hide that from him if she took it in the van."

"That's what is so puzzling about this. But there's more. Constable Brown was apparently monitoring the activities of this oil sands protest group. That seems to have been the reason for his visit to Fort McKay. His responsibility was to prevent any damage to persons or property."

"Could he have learned by accident that Beverly was missing while he was there?"

"Yes, Beverly's mother told him when he asked to talk to her daughter that she didn't know where she was, and that she was worried about her."

31

Inspector St. James asked Beth and Claire to watch the interrogation of Jeff Stevens, which was being filmed using CCTV. They were sitting in another room in front of a television screen at the RCMP building in Fort McMurray. In the interview room, Sergeant Reynaldo was sitting across from the security guard at a spartan rectangular wood table. "Did you know Beverly Racette? And when did you last see her?"

"I met her at The Lodge, we had a few drinks together, then she asked me to show her the oil sands. I said OK, and I told her to duck down when I drove through the main gate. There was no one much around. I showed her where I worked. There's an office with living quarters reserved for security guards. That's all."

"Then what happened?"

"Well, I started to cuddle up with her, and she said no, and started yelling. I tried to calm her, but it didn't work. Then she ran out of the building. I tried to follow her, but I couldn't find her among the buildings in the complex. So I went back to the security office. My shift didn't start for another hour, so I lay down on the bed and fell asleep. I figured that she'd come back to get a ride back to The Lodge from the mine, but she never did."

"What did she have with her? A rucksack, for instance, or something else?"

"No, nothing."

"What about a cell phone?"

"Not that I could see."

"Did she tell you what she thought of the oil sands?"

"Only that she was doing a class project about them."

"You realize that she was no longer in school?"

"Uh, no. The only things I know about her are what she told me."

*****

Beth frowned, and said to Inspector St. James: "We still don't know what happened to her cell phone. If it wasn't on the body when it was found, then it may still be at the site."

"I've sent the forensic people to go over the ground and the tailings pond where she was found. If it's not there, then someone took it."

"What still doesn't add up is why he and his partner got transferred to another job site. He presumably didn't tell anyone what happened. Then why did his employer move him to Mildred Lake? The timing of it suggests it can't be a coincidence."

"Good question. We need to talk again to Howard Thomas at the Wildcat Oil Services office, as well as to his staff."

"Who is this 'we'?"

"I was hoping you could come with me."

"As long as Constable Brown isn't there."

"That's right, he won't." He smiled at her. "You know, I can see you'll make a very fine detective. Too bad you don't work for the RCMP!"

*****

Beth and Inspector St. James sat facing the local boss of Wildcat Oil Services in his office again. "Now, Mr. Thomas, we would like the truth about the reason Jeff Stevens and his partner were transferred to Mildred Lake a few days after Beverly Racette was found dead in the tailings pond. I should mention that Stevens has admitted to smuggling her into the mine complex and making sexual advances."

Thomas cringed. "OK, I admit that it wasn't just a routine rotation of the two pairs of security guards. Constable Brown came to see me. He's been coordinating with me in monitoring the protests against the oil sands operations, since WOS is involved in security. He had heard a rumour that one of my guards had gone too far in trying to prevent outsiders from gathering information about the mining operations. He wasn't specific, but we thought it would avoid trouble if I rotated him out of there. Since the guards work in pairs, I did the same for his partner."

<h1 style="text-align:center">32</h1>

Beth was in the RCMP Detachment building, speaking to Inspector St. James. "Do you really think that an 18-year-old girl was a threat to the oil sands? Is there any evidence that the group she was affiliated with had any plans to commit violence or to sabotage the operation there?"

St. James met her gaze warily. "Not directly, no. But we're always on the lookout for terrorist activity. You can't expect us to turn a blind eye to protest movements. We need to be aware of what they're planning."

"So Constable Brown was told to keep an eye on them?"

"That is one of his duties, yes."

"Does that include talking to a security firm that is patrolling the oil sands site?"

"It could."

Beth frowned. "Constable Brown alerted the boss at the WOS office here that something had happened at the Muskeg River Mine that would get their guards into trouble, and that was why Thomas chose to transfer them to Mildred Lake. Surely, that's going beyond Brown's responsibilities! In fact, it's abetting a crime!"

St. James hesitated before replying. "According to him, the guard had been too zealous in preventing unauthorized access, but it wasn't necessarily criminal."

"What is more troubling is the possibility that Brown knew about the death of an indigenous woman, but did nothing about it until we reported spotting the body in the drone footage. It suggests that the reputation of the oil sands companies was more important than justice for the First Nations."

St. James bridled. "I would dispute that. Nevertheless, I will order an inquiry into the events at the Muskeg River Mine and our response to it."

*****

"Beth, how are you getting on with your activities there in Fort McMurray?" Sean said when they next spoke on the phone. "If you don't come home I'm going to come out and see for myself!"

"OK, OK, come on out here then! I'm just trying to get some justice for indigenous women. As I explained before, an 18-year-old died and the RCMP has done little to find out how it happened."

"I thought you were campaigning against the oil sands. Now you've taken up the cause of indigenous women?"

"The two are related. Anyway, I've got to go. Email me your travel plans and I'll arrange to pick you up at the airport here."

*****

Beth introduced Sean to her friends. "This is Claire, Tom Boswell's daughter. She and I have been doing some sleuthing, together with Flora." He shook hands with the two women, who were waiting at the hotel when Beth and Sean arrived from the airport. "Let's go to Earls Kitchen and have a meal after you check into your room."

Sean looked around as they walked to Earls. "I'll bet you'll be glad to get back to Nova Scotia, Beth! I'm surprised you've stayed out here so long!"

"Oh, I don't know. It sort of grows on you," Beth replied. "I like the people here, the wide open spaces. They're worth fighting for!" Claire and Flora nodded.

Seeing he was outnumbered, Sean fell silent.

The meal wasn't the joyful reunion he'd anticipated. *Maybe it's the jet lag,* he thought. After walking back to the hotel, he crashed in his room and slept for 9 hours, awakening at six the next morning. He went for a walk along the Athabasca River. *I still can't get used to this place. There aren't enough trees. It's too flat! And too far from the ocean!*

He met Beth at eight for breakfast. She told him about the latest developments in the investigation of Beverly's death. "At least the RCMP is going to examine whether Constable Brown acted properly. Maybe this will lead the Force to take more seriously the violence against indigenous women and concentrate less on the protests against the oil sands."

"Beth, you've gotten far away from the purpose of your trip to Fort McMurray, which was to locate Jeremy Boswell's cousin. You did fine on that job, but then you turned Jeremy against Tom by harping on the evils of the oil sands. Apparently you didn't realize that Jeremy was a big supporter of the industry when he worked at a venture capital firm, and a major stockholder in his own right of Wildcat Oil Services itself!"

"Well, just because we are hired by someone doesn't mean that we have to adopt their values, does it? That reminds me—why didn't Jeremy know that Tom worked for WOS? Why did he have to hire us to find him?"

"It's just one of those coincidences, I guess. A lot of people moved from Nova Scotia to Alberta to work in the oil sands. Jeremy knew Ruben Gallant, and maybe also Howard Thomas. Unbeknownst to him, his cousin Tom Boswell was also out here. Jeremy wouldn't have known any of the junior people at WOS so he wouldn't have been aware of it."

"I guess it makes sense."

"So, what's next, Beth?"

"You know, I think I'd like to just stay out here. I feel it's where I belong. If I move back east, I'll miss my gal pals, Claire and Flora."

"But what would you do for a living? You realize Cameron and Carroll can't continue to pay you! You'd have to resign and find another job." He shook his head.

"I've been kicking around in my mind the idea that I could work as a detective here in Alberta. There's a lot more that needs to be done to bring justice to the indigenous peoples. I feel I can make a difference."

"That's all very well and good, but is there any local detective agency here that does that work that can take you on?"

"Not that I'm aware of, which makes it all the more important for someone to start doing it. Claire, Flora, and I have begun exploring the idea of forming our own detective agency. We'd concentrate on investigating issues relating to the First

Nations and the oil sands. There's a need for someone to do that."

Sean shook his head sadly. "I was afraid you were going to say something like that. But I must admit that you've blossomed as a detective. You don't back down, you keep at it until you solve a case. I'm sure you'll do well if your detective agency gets off the ground."

Beth brightened. "I'm glad to hear that from you. You don't mind too much?"

"I had the feeling that this might happen, but I can't say I'm happy about it. That's life. Anyway, what are your short-term plans?"

"Flora said I could share her place for a while, until I found a place of my own. I'll fly back to Nova Scotia in a few weeks to arrange to move out of my Dartmouth apartment. I'll ship the stuff I need back here, and sell or give away the rest."

33

St. James invited Claire and Beth to his office in the RCMP's Fort McMurray building. "I wanted to tell you what happened when we searched the site where Beverly Racette was found. Our investigators used a metal detector to see if there was anything that we missed the first time. That's how we found her phone, which had been buried in the bitumen by the tires of the 400 tonne haulers. It must have fallen out of her pocket at some point."

"What was on her phone? Have you been able to get it to work?" Beth asked.

"The phone works, but we need Beverly's pin to get access. We're at a dead end."

Claire spoke up. "Can you leave it with us for a day or two? Our contacts on the reserve might be able to help us. I don't think they would be willing to cooperate with the RCMP directly, but we should at least be able to discover whether there's evidence on her phone as to what happened to her and let you know."

"I guess so. But make sure you don't modify the contents of the phone in any way."

*****

Claire called Sadie. "Do you know the pin for Beverly's phone? The RCMP found the phone, but can't unlock it to see what's on it."

"I might, but I really don't want them to have access. They would be able to read all our emails and text messages, and probably would charge me with some crime or other related to our crusade against the oil sands! And it would compromise the other organizations that are fighting to save the planet from environmental destruction!"

"Tell you what, Sadie, if I lend you the phone, would you look through the pics to see if she took any at the Muskeg River Mine? It's important to know whether there are any clues about how she died. If there are, then we need to figure out how to give them to the RCMP without allowing them full access to the phone."

"All right. I'll be in Fort McMurray again tomorrow and I'll try to unlock it."

*****

Sadie was sitting opposite Claire and Beth at the NGO's trailer. "I think I remember the pin for accessing Beverly's phone. We didn't have secrets from each other, and sometimes she would ask me to boot up her phone and check her emails or to look at a pic. Yes! I've gotten into it. Let me look at the photo gallery. Wow! There are some photos of the oil sands, dated the day she went to The Lodge."

"Can I see?" Beth asked. "Oh, I recognize that place. That's next to the hanger where the big haulage Cats are kept–where Claire and I got taken by George."

Claire looked over Sadie's shoulder. "Here are a few pics of the oil sands themselves. Look at the giant scars in the land! Here's one with the tailings pond in the background, near to where she was found. It looks as though it's been taken from some vehicle or other. The view is from the road where we found the tire marks that match those of the guards' van. It's still light out."

"That's all the recent pics there are on her phone. They don't tell us much, though we do have the exact time they were taken so we do know when she was there." Beth scratched her head. "If Beverly took the pics from Stevens' van, then he obviously knew she had a camera. And why would he have assumed that she wanted to 'cuddle,' as he put it? She would have had to explain that her interest was in documenting the oil sands. Something doesn't add up here."

Sadie looked disappointed. "Too bad we didn't find a smoking gun. And I'm not going to give the unlock code to the RCMP! Perhaps we could just email those photos to them, and say that I refuse to give them the code?"

"I'll check with my boss, Hamish Cameron, who is a retired judge, but I think you can argue that being forced to give the pin to the RCMP would violate your right against self-incrimination. It may not be your phone, but since you shared its use with Beverly and it contains things personal to you, you can't be accused of withholding evidence. That's what I'll tell the RCMP, anyway. We'll have to give them back the phone, and they may be able to unlock it anyway using another technique. But I think St. James will take my word that it doesn't contain any more information about Beverly's visit to the oil sands."

*****

St. James was comfortable with the arrangement, and he thanked Beth for the photos from Beverly's phone that she had sent him. "I looked at them, and I agree that they don't jibe with what Jeff Stevens told us before. I've asked Sergeant Reynaldo to interview the suspect again. You can join me and watch it on CCTV."

The Sergeant was sitting across from Stevens in the interview room. "Now Jeff, would you go into more detail about what Beverly did after you smuggled her into the Muskeg River Mine? Did you show her the site and drive her down to the tailings pond in your van? Did she take any pictures?"

"No, we didn't go down there. She didn't take any pics while she was with me. She must have gone down there after running away."

"You realize that we have Beverly's phone, and that she took a picture of the sands not far from where her body was found in the tailings pond. It looks as though the picture was taken from a vehicle. There are tire marks nearby along the road that match those of your security van. What do you have to say to that?"

Stevens suddenly looked very tired.

"I couldn't let her take pictures. If someone saw her, WOS would fire me like a shot. I tried to grab her arm, but she managed to slip out of my grasp. She jumped out the door and ran along the haulage road back toward the entrance gate. I sprinted after her, and was about to catch her when she tripped and fell. Her head hit something, perhaps a boulder dropped by one of the trucks. She lay there on the ground without moving. I felt her pulse. Nothing. I didn't know what to do!" He put his head down on his arms and started sobbing.

"OK, then what? Did you call for medical help?"

"How could I? I would have lost my job! I went back to the van and drove it to where she was lying. I put her in the back, and drove along the haulage road until I got close to the tailings pond. I pulled off the road. Then I dragged her to the edge of the pond and rolled her into the water." He shuddered. "It was awful, but I had to do it."

"You sure she wasn't still alive?"

"Nah, it's impossible! I told ya, she didn't have a pulse!"

"Jeff, I have to warn you, we've exhumed the body. It turns out that she died of drowning. You're at least going to be charged with manslaughter, and possibly with murder. Your actions directly brought about her death."

"But I'm innocent. It was an accident!"

"You have the right to hire a lawyer and to defend yourself." Reynaldo paused for a few moments. "In the meantime, you can help yourself by telling us who you told about this, and why you were transferred to Mildred Lake."

Stevens shook his head hopelessly. "I knew I couldn't stay there. So I told my partner, Al, what had happened and that I wanted to leave. He promised to do something about it. He talked to Constable Brown, who had heard of plots by activists on the reserve to disrupt the oil sands operation. Al told him that we had discovered a teenage indigenous woman trying to sabotage the haulage trucks at the site. As we attempted to catch her, she had fallen to her death in the tailings pond. Brown agreed that it was best not to publicize this, that we should keep quiet about it. He would explain to Mr. Thomas, our boss at WOS, what had happened and let him decide what to do.

"The next day Thomas told us to pack our bags and check in at Mildred Lake."

*****

"We interrupt the six o'clock news with a breaking story here in Edmonton. The RCMP's Deputy Commissioner for Alberta has called a news conference to give an update of its investigation of the death of a Fort McKay indigenous woman. To remind our viewers, Beverly Racette, aged 18, was found dead in a tailings pond at the Muskeg River Mine there four weeks ago. The Deputy Commissioner has admitted that the Force has not treated the case with the seriousness that it deserved, and in fact, tried to cover up the incident. One of its constables, who was not named, has been disciplined as a result. The Force has determined that a security guard working for Wildcat Oil Services at the site was responsible for her death, and he will be brought to trial. Moreover, the RCMP has referred the actions of the oil services company to the Alberta Energy Regulator, which will rule on the fitness of the company to continue to be licensed in the province."

*****

Beth, Claire, and Flora were sitting together at a wine bar in downtown Fort McMurray, watching the news broadcast. "We did it," Beth said with tears in her eyes. "At least some justice will be done for poor Beverly."

Claire shook her head. "Let's wait and see how it plays out. We've got to keep at it, or otherwise they'll go back to their old ways."

"You know, *amigas*, this has been a great experience for me," Flora added. "I don't want it to stop. Can't we keep fighting for justice for indigenous women and against environmental destruction?"

Beth nodded her head in agreement. "You're right, there's a lot left to do. And I don't want to go back to Nova Scotia. I like it here, despite the lousy air quality."

Claire was enthusiastic. "You know, we could form a detective agency, the three of us, like the one you work for, Beth!" Turning to Flora, she said, "We could call it the *Tres Amigas!*"

"Is there any money in it?" Flora asked. "I'm going to need some *dinero* to live on, and to send back to relatives. I won't be able to keep my job at WOS after all that's happened, and I'm not sure I want to work for the oil industry anyway."

Beth considered the question. "I haven't been a detective long enough to know how profitable it is. I guess it all depends on whether we can attract rich clients or not. Someone like Jeremy Boswell." She paused for a few seconds, then continued. "I have another idea. Maybe we could team up with some lawyers and investigate the health issues related to the mining of the oil sands. This could lead to a class-action suit against the oil companies–like what I pretended to do when I approached Tom, Claire's father!"

Claire nodded her head in support of the idea. "Fighting climate change and addressing health issues are causes that many people–including rich donors–can relate to. As a result, the

NGOs in those areas are pretty well heeled, They can afford to hire legal services, and I imagine they could afford to hire detectives as well. Plus the Fort McKay First Nation has a substantial share of the oil sands revenues. They could use them to hire us to monitor the oil companies to make sure they live up to their agreements with the First Nation. I'll ask the Chief on the reserve what he thinks."

Beth added: "We would need to be licensed here in Alberta and complete an investigator training course first. But at least we have a good relationship with Inspector St. James. I think he takes us seriously now."

Flora nodded to the other two. "Hmm, this might work, but we need to weigh the possibilities carefully before jumping in. We have to do some market research. Let's put together a plan and see what our prospects are."

The three of them raised their glasses. "To the *Tres Amigas!*"

34

Calgary and Halifax

Izzie and Hamish marvelled at the majestic scenery. The air was fresh and clear, the fall foliage magnificent. "This is close to paradise, isn't it," Izzie cooed.

"I can understand Beth wants to live out here in Alberta. Though personally I'd much rather live in Banff than in Fort McMurray!"

Hamish's phone rang. "I should have turned the damn thing off! That's life these days–no more peace and quiet! I guess I'll answer anyway."

"Hamish, this is Francis. The electoral commission has ruled in my favour, so I'm back on the hustings! Wildcat Oil Services has been censured and told not to interfere in politics or elections. It is prohibited from doing any more lobbying in British Columbia."

"That's great! So our efforts have been successful. It shows that money isn't everything!"

"Thanks for your and Izzie's help. Why don't you come visit me in Surrey? I'll give you the keys to my riding, metaphorically speaking!"

"It's very tempting, but we've been away from home for too long. It's time to go back."

*****

"It's been a pretty good trip," Hamish said to Izzie as the plane taxied to the terminal at Halifax's Stanfield airport. "You got to attend your conference in Victoria, and I met an old friend there whom I hadn't seen in a long time. We had the opportunity to tour around some of BC and Alberta, including visiting Fort McMurray, which we would never otherwise have seen. It was also nice to get some work done to protect our democratic institutions."

"I just read in the *Globe* that Francis Lee has been re-elected, after being cleared of violating BC's election act so he could run again. He has us to thank for that."

"It was good to see that Beth is doing fine. She managed to find Tom Boswell for Jeremy, and helped bring the two of them together. It's not her fault that they didn't hit it off. I think she's found her calling and is going to do great things with her life. I just wonder whether that will include Sean. I don't know how he'll take it if it doesn't."

35

Ashcroft-by-the-Sea

Hamish found Sean at home when he returned to The Oaks. He could see that his partner in the Cameron and Carroll, Investigators, was depressed about something. After the usual greetings, Hamish asked, "What's happening now with the detective agency? Are there any new cases that Beth could work on?"

Sean explained to Hamish the outcome of his trip to Fort McMurray. "Beth has decided to stay in Alberta and start a detective agency with Claire and Flora. At least for the moment they're going to work out of the office of the NGO, AOSCP, where Claire is employed now. Once they get licensed by the province, they're going to call themselves the *Tres Amigas!* Apparently they have a contract already with the Fort McKay First Nation monitoring the actions of the oil companies on their ancestral lands. So much for our hiring a junior detective to share some of the workload! Beth didn't stay long."

"That's too bad. I was starting to like her. And she learned the ropes quickly. In fact, she taught us a few things."

"Like what?"

"To stick up for the little guy–or gal. And not to give up just because the other side is floating on a sea of money."

Sean shook his head sadly. "I'm going to miss her. But she's got most of her life ahead of her while mine is mostly in the rear-view mirror."

"Ha! You're a couple of decades younger than I am! Which leads me to the thought that you and Marjoree should get together again, now that you and Beth are no longer an item. You make a good couple, and you could still have many good times together."

Sean looked glum. "I don't know if she would take me back. Anyway, I've decided I need a change of scenery. I want to take some time off to get over Beth."

"Oh, and what would that involve?"

"I'd like to take a sabbatical from the detective agency, and also to get away from Ashcroft for a while. I'm considering living on my sailboat."

Hamish thought: *A man usually runs away to sea because of a woman. Either she broke his heart, or he married her!* To Sean, he said, "Oh, yeah? Seriously? That's a big step. And who's going to run the detective agency? I was the one who wanted to ease out–remember? If you leave, I'm not going to handle Cameron and Carroll alone! Go on, talk to Marjoree. Eat some humble pie. At least try to get her to manage our detective office again, now that Beth is out of the picture. See what she says."

*****

Marjoree was surprised to hear the doorbell of her town-house. *Who's that, I wonder?* When she opened the door, she saw Sean, who was sheepishly standing on the top step.

"Marjoree, can I come in? I have some explaining to do."

"You certainly do! But come on in, no point doing your explaining on my doorstep."

She refrained from inviting him into the living room. Rather, she pointed to one of the straight back chairs around the dining table. "Excuse me if I don't offer you any refreshment," she said sarcastically. "Now, what do you have to say?"

"This whole thing with Beth was a mistake. Hamish was right about that. I expect she saw me as a way out from her dead-end job. It's over between us."

"Oh yeah? And what about you? Did you see her as a way out of our dead-end relationship?"

"I let myself be charmed by a younger woman. I've learned my lesson."

"So, you're blaming it all on her, are you? What are you, some sort of spineless ageing teenager who lets his hormones rule his life?"

"Now, don't be that way, Marjoree! I said I was sorry. Anyway, I'm planning to live on my sailboat for a bit, to try and get my head back in order."

"And what about the detective agency? You can't expect Hamish to handle it on his own, and I'm guessing Beth isn't coming back. If you take off, then Cameron and Carroll is kaput."

"Well, it would only be for a few months. In the meantime, you could help Hamish run the detective agency. There's not that much time for me to do any sailing before winter sets in anyway. I have another idea: What about going sailing with me from time to time this fall? There are a lot of coves and bays to explore along here. What do you say?"

"So you're asking me to go back to the way we were before? Too many things have happened since then for that. Anyway, you don't seem to know what you want. It's true that I miss sailing. It brings back good memories of the times John and I spent on his forty footer, which, I will point out, was considerably larger and more comfortable than your boat. Ask me some time, I'll see if I want to go sailing with you or not. Let's leave it at that." Marjoree got up, and shepherded Sean to the door.

He reluctantly left, like a dog with its tail between its legs.

36

"Hamish, this is Jeremy Boswell. Can I come by and have a word with you and Sean? I could stop by The Oaks this afternoon, if that's convenient."

"Of course, Jeremy. I'll be here, though Sean is out doing other things."

Though Boswell was considerably younger than Hamish, he seemed more frail and wizened than his host. He had aged in the few months since he had hired Cameron and Carroll, Investigators. His bent frame and bony face did not suggest that he would live many more years.

"Come in, come in," Hamish said. "Here, have a seat on the sofa. Tell me what's on your mind."

"You probably know that I didn't much enjoy the reunion with my cousin Tom in Fort McMurray. We left each other on bad terms. The trip out to Alberta was a disaster."

"Yes, I heard about it. Why was that?"

"I was dismayed by their criticism of the oil sands. I've been a supporter–and an investor–for a long time. Their vehemence surprised and offended me, since I have long thought that our successful exploitation of the deposits is something that Canada should be proud of. But since then I have had a change of heart. I've done my own research of the oil sands, and talked to people with intimate knowledge of their environmental effects on the native peoples in the area. I recognize now that the criticisms by environmentalists are largely valid. So I'd like you to apologize to Beth and ask her to help me get back in touch once again with my cousin and his daughter."

"That's big of you to admit you were wrong. I'd be happy to talk to Beth about it if that eases the way."

"In hindsight, I'm glad I got a chance to meet Tom again. He's led a generally fulfilling life, even if it hasn't been an easy one. The ecological damage from mining the oil sands contributed to that, affecting his health and cutting short his wife's life. Upon reflection, I've decided to try to make things better by endowing an independent institute to do research into how to exploit the oil sands in a more sustainable way."

"That seems like a noble endeavor! What do you have in mind, exactly?"

"The institute will be devoted to research on minimizing the health risks from atmospheric and water-borne pollution, finding more environmentally-friendly processes for extraction and processing, and perfecting carbon capture and storage. These are of course things that are already being studied, including by the oil companies themselves, but we will be independent of them and not open to accusations of greenwashing. We'll be able to finance cutting-edge research. I intend to make the institute one of the leaders in environmental science applied to oil sector issues. "

"So your aim is to enable continued development of the oil sands while lessening its negative impacts. How did you get the idea of an independent research institute?"

"I talked about financing research in the area with the head of WOS, Ruben Gallant, thinking we could collaborate, but after several discussions with him I decided to go it alone. We've known each other for a long time, but now we're no longer on the same page. He's too interested in selling the oil sands to the public rather than in making them more eco-friendly. I've learned that he has been deliberately circulating false information and trying to influence elections by covert means and dirty tricks."

"I gather that the Alberta Energy Regulator is considering whether to continue to license his company. There is still some doubt whether the Fort McMurray office of WOS was acting ethically in spying on the protesters against oil sands development. Moreover, the manager there is accused of helping to cover up Beverly's death. The RCMP is pursuing its investigation."

"That's right. In my view there's an urgent need for the oil industry to clean up its act. It has to face the reality that the way it exploits the oil sands is a blot on Canada's reputation. It's going to have to change for us to meet our zero carbon emission targets, and it needs to pay greater attention to the health risks from its operations."

"I'm surprised to hear you say that, but I think you're right."

"I'm going to do what I can to make things better. Construction of the Boswell Institute building is due to start this year in Calgary. I'm donating my WOS shares to a foundation that will fund the project. I hope to hire staff in the meantime so that the institute can be up and running as soon as the building is complete. I plan to ask my cousin Tom whether he wants to join the staff there. His experience in the industry would be very useful."

*****

When Sean returned, Hamish told him of his conversation with Jeremy Boswell. "He's had a change of heart, and he's decided to fund a research institute to study how to make exploitation of the oil sands more sustainable. He wants to get together with Tom and Claire again. I'm going to contact Beth and ask her to facilitate a reconciliation with Jeremy."

"I'm sure Tom and Claire will be grateful for that, even if they don't make it into Jeremy's will."

"Who knows? At least they're going to be on speaking terms now, thanks to Beth's efforts. I suspect that Beth will develop some relationship with the Boswell Institute as well, if as expected the *Tres Amigas* gets involved in environmental issues."

"So that's tied up another loose end. I'm starting to think that our work at the detective agency is coming to a natural close. It will be a good time for me to bow out for a time."

37

On Trahearne Bay

Sean and Marjoree set out from Ashcroft Yacht Club in moderate winds and clear skies to enjoy a beautiful fall morning on the water. After a few hours of tacking aimlessly back and forth on Sean's CS 30 sailboat, they returned to the yacht club where they tied up at his slip. "Let's have lunch at the bar. We can sit outside and enjoy the sunshine," Sean suggested.

They installed themselves at one of the outdoor tables. "What can I get you?" Sean asked, as he got up to give their orders to the bartender.

He brought back a pair of *kirs royales*, their favourite drink, made with sparkling white wine and blackberry liqueur. "To your and my continued good health, and to many years of pleasant sailing!"

Marjoree clicked their glasses, but with a sceptical expression on her face. "Let's not get ahead of ourselves here, Sean."

"Actually, I wanted to bounce a plan off you. You and I could sail south, escape the winter, and do some serious cruising on my boat starting this fall. Why not do what a lot of couples do when they retire: live on a sailboat in the sun for a few months, or maybe even years. No deadlines, no more work weeks, no definite plans! Let's just decide on a destination, stay for a while, and pull up the anchor when it takes our fancy!"

"Hold on a minute, Sean. How is that going to work? Don't forget that to get anywhere from Nova Scotia, you're going to have to do some sailing on the open ocean. Are you sure that your boat is big enough? John had a saying, *Blue water sailing is playing Russian roulette with Mother Nature. Somewhere out there is a wave with your name on it, and it will find you.* It's not going to be all sunshine and calm seas!"

"I've worked it all out. We would go down the South Shore, cut over to the Cape Cod Canal, go west along the Long Island Sound, and then take the Intracoastal Waterway south all the way to Florida. Only the first part would be over open water, and if the weather didn't cooperate we could always duck into a harbour along the New England coast. Once past New York we could stop at any number of scenic little towns along the inland waterway. Visit places like St. Michaels, Oxford, and Reedville on Chesapeake Bay, Elizabeth City after going through the Dismal Swamp Canal, and the two Beauforts (one in North Carolina, the other in South Carolina), Charleston, and many others. Watch the missile launches from Cape Canaveral, sightsee in St. Augustine, Palm Beach, and Fort Lauderdale! There are plenty of Canadian boats that take that intracoastal route, many having come down from Lake Ontario through New York's canals and the Hudson River. If we leave in the next few weeks we can be far enough south to avoid much of the winter. Then we can see how it goes–take our time, play it by ear."

"Hmm, this is all very sudden. You can't just drop every-thing and run off to sea. There's the detective agency to worry about, and our houses that would need to be taken care of somehow–whether they are rented out or someone hired to look after them. Most people I know, who've done what you describe, plan it for at least a year or two before going on an extended cruise."

38

Ashcroft-by-the-Sea

Sean returned to The Oaks and told Hamish about his conversation with Marjoree. "She hasn't said 'yes' yet, but at least she hasn't said 'no'."

Hamish reacted with disbelief. "So now you're planning not just to live on your boat here in Nova Scotia, but also take it down to Florida. Would you do that even if Marjoree didn't agree to accompany you? And how long would you be away in either case?"

"Well, that's the beauty of it. I wouldn't need to decide on an itinerary or a timetable. I would play it by ear. But my route would be pretty much the same one as the one other boats take. There's a guide book and charts for every place along the way. It's a great way to see the sights along the east coast."

"Well, good luck with that! Are you sure that you've thought it through? It's a pretty big change in your lifestyle! You'll be moving from a house on land to one that is one tenth the size of your existing one and floats on water. If the anchor drags, the boat–that is, your house–may end up on the rocks, so in bad weather you'll stay up in the middle of the night to mount an anchor watch. You'll be hostage to storms like never before in your life, and you'll have to spend much of your time foraging for food to stay alive, fuel for your boat's engine, and laundromats to wash your clothes!"

Sean hunched his shoulders. "I won't know if the cruising life suits me until I try it. It's true that one can always benefit from doing more preparation. I could address a lot of issues with more time, including deciding what to provision and making sure that I have the spare parts I may need. There are so many systems on board–more than in your average house: stoves, batteries, heaters, fridges, navigation equipment, vhf radios, solar and wind power chargers, plumbing, sails, engines, bilge pumps, and so on, all of which can be expected to break down at some point. Most of them have parts that need to be specially ordered. It's better not to rely on finding them along the way, but deciding which spares to take is difficult because there's not much storage space on the boat–you just have room for the essentials."

"So you've decided to put it off for a year or two?"

"No, because too much preparation can be bad too. It may lead one to get cold feet and abandon the project. Some long-time cruisers say: 'Just go!' If you get caught up in the details you may never leave, and miss out on the experience of a lifetime."

"That brings up another question or two, Sean. What shall we do about the agency? And if you did go away for an extended period, what would you do with your house?"

"Of course you could stay here, Hamish. I certainly wouldn't want to leave it empty. And I would keep in touch. After all, in today's world physical proximity is no longer as essential as it once was. I might even be able to continue to do detective work from my boat!"

*****

Marjorie came around to Sean's argument in favour of a quick departure in order to beat the winter. "I guess if we're going to go cruising south, this is the best time to leave. I've found a tenant for my townhouse, and a realtor friend is going to manage the property. I have no worries. As for stuff we forget to bring, we can always shop along the way. We're not setting off across the Atlantic! We'll learn little by little what we need to keep on the boat, and provision at various ports along the waterway."

"With Hamish staying in The Oaks, I leave it in good hands. Actually, Izzie has decided to divide her time between Ashcroft and Halifax to keep Hamish company., I couldn't ask for better tenants."

*****

The big day was scheduled for a Saturday at the end of September. Sean and Marjorie's friends turned up at the yacht club early in the morning to see them off: many of them AYC members, but also Hamish and Izzie, Andy, and Joe Washington.

After Marjoree had untied the dock lines and brought them aboard, Sean backed *Spray* out of her slip and headed out from the marina into the coastal waters of Nova Scotia's South Shore, waving farewell to his well wishers on the dock. After he and Marjoree raised the mainsail and rolled out the jib, they turned south with a lively west wind pushing them along at a steady six knots.

About the Author

More information about my detective series, *The ABC Files*, can be found on my website, <u>paulmassonwebsite.com</u>. I would welcome your feedback: you can email me using the "Contact Me" form there, or if you would like to receive advance notice of new novels and a prequel of the ABC Files.

I am a retired economist living in Niagara-on-the-Lake, Ontario, and have published extensively on various aspects of international economics and macroeconomic policy. My hobbies include hiking, gardening, kayaking, and sailing. My sailboat, *Fugue*, is berthed at the Niagara-on-the-Lake Sailing Club.

My detective novels can be found on Amazon, Goodreads, and bookshop.org, and booksellers can order them from IngramSpark. If you enjoyed this book, please consider submitting a review.

www.ingramcontent.com/pod-product-compliance
Lightning Source LLC
Chambersburg PA
CBHW031959180726
48283CB00008B/2500